"This book is a practical gui[de...]
Jeff written a helpful book, h[...]
is an excellent resource for [...]
ents helping singles achieve [...]

Christ For The Nations

"Because Jesus lived as the greatest example of a single man, He would have promoted this book for everyone to read, single or married. Jeff has written an anointed book that will empower you to get your eyes off your personal needs and focus on the great destiny God has for you."

Randy Bozarth
Vice President, Christ For The Nations

"This book is a great tool to help singles navigate through difficult relationship issues! Fantastic for singles pastors who want to produce a holy generation."

Daniel Guajardo
Spiritual Life Administrator, Oral Roberts University

"In a day when people have largely strayed from the pathway that leads to developing strong loving relationships, that stand the test of time, this book comes as a breath of fresh air. It presents the single person with practical advice in dealing with the innumerable emotions and frustrations that all too often precede marriage. The stories and biblical principals bring great hope and comfort."

Mario Mariani
Pastor of Lytham Christian Centre, England

"Jeff Hidden is a great communicator and what he communicates in his practical and down-to-earth way changes lives. For the many singles caught in the trap of peer-pressure, rejection and frustration, this book gives the way out. It is a book I will be recommending in the UK."

Hugh Osgood
Senior Minister, Cornerstone Christian Centre, London; President and Chair of Council, Churches in Communities International.

"As a pastor for over 51 years, I never realized the frustration singles go through in waiting for "Mr. or Mrs. Right". This book is great for singles; however, it's much more than that. It is great for pastors, counselors, and Christian leaders, to better understand how to minister to singles."

Don Lyon
Apostle, Faith Center

"After leading one of the oldest singles ministries for 27 years, it is so refreshing and such a blessing to see the insight Jeff has in this book. It points to who we are in Christ rather than thinking marriage solves all our problems."

Gerry Gallicchio
President, Singles Reaching Singles

"This book is full of practical questions and thoughts people have regarding why they have not married yet. Jeff gives well-thought-through responses to these questions, balanced with related scriptures and sample prayers single adults can use in talking with God about the whole issue."

Dennis Franck
Director, Assemblies of God Single Adult Ministries

"God has blessed Jeff with a unique understanding of interpersonal relationships. This book has a clear message tremendously appropriate for the heart cry of millions of singles. I found myself saying, "Yes, yes!" all through it. Jeff has a marvelous way of presenting deep topics in a simple manner that keeps you meditating on them for hours."

John Whitmire
Engineer; divorcee; Director, Singles Reaching Singles

"I read this book in one sitting; it was right on target!"

Jennifer Harry
Single Adult

"The principles in this book are life changing. My divorce was unwanted and unexpected. This book helped me tremendously."

Kristen Morris
Single again

I THOUGHT FOR SURE I'D BE MARRIED BY NOW

A Powerful Guide to Help Singles Enjoy the Journey

Jeff Hidden

ACW Press
Ozark, AL 36360

Except where otherwise indicated all Scripture quotations are taken from the New King James Version, Copyright © 1979, 1980, 1982 by Thomas Nelson, Inc., Publishers. Used by permission.

Verses marked KJV are taken from the King James Version of the Bible.

Verses marked NASB are taken from the New American Standard Bible®, Copyright © 1960, 1962, 1963, 1968, 1971, 1972, 1973, 1975, 1977, 1995 by The Lockman Foundation. Used by permission.

Verses marked AMP are taken from The Amplified Bible, Old Testament, Copyright © 1965 and 1987 by The Zondervan Corporation, and from The Amplified Bible, New Testament, Copyright © 1954, 1958, 1987 by The Lockman Foundation. Used by permission.

Verses marked NIV are taken from the Holy Bible, New International Version®. Copyright © 1973, 1978, 1984 by the International Bible Society. Used by permission of Zondervan Publishing House. The "NIV" and "New International Version" trademarks are registered in the United States Patent and Trademark Office by International Bible Society.

Verses marked THE MESSAGE are taken from THE MESSAGE. Copyright © by Eugene H. Peterson 1993, 1994, 1995. Used by permission of NavPress Publishing Group.

I Thought for Sure I'd Be Married by Now!
Copyright ©2005 Jeff Hidden
All rights reserved

Cover Design by Alpha Advertising
Interior design by Pine Hill Graphics

Packaged by ACW Press
1200 Hwy 231 South #273
Ozark, AL 36360
www.acwpress.com
The views expressed or implied in this work do not necessarily reflect those of ACW Press. Ultimate design, content, and editorial accuracy of this work is the responsibility of the author(s).

Publisher's Cataloging-in-Publication Data
(Provided by Cassidy Cataloguing Services, Inc.)

Hidden, Jeff.

I thought for sure I'd be married by now : a powerful guide to help singles enjoy the journey / Jeff Hidden. -- 1st ed. -- Ozark, AL : ACW Press, 2004.

p. ; cm.
ISBN: 1-932124-44-6

1. Single people--Religious life. 2. Man-woman relationships--Religious aspects. 3. Dating (Social customs)--Religious aspects. 4. Mate selection--Religious aspects. 5. Interpersonal relations--Religious aspects. 6. Christian life. I. Title.

BV4596.S5 H53 2004
248.8/4--dc22   0410

All rights reserved. No part of this book may be reproduced, stored in a retrieval system, or transmitted in any form or by any means—electronic, mechanical, photocopying, recording, or otherwise—without prior permission in writing from the copyright holder except as provided by USA copyright law.

Printed in the United States of America.

DEDICATION

To every "Single" person
who has ever struggled
with his or her singleness
and especially to those
who thought for sure
they would be married by now.

Contents

Acknowledgements 9
Introduction 11

Section I—The Big Picture
1. Are We There Yet? 17

Section II—Don't Worry; Be Happy!
2. Do Not Fret 27
3. The Power of Thank-You Prayers 33
4. A Typical Day's Journey 41

Section III—Trusting God
5. You're in Good Hands 51
6. When, God, When? 55

Section IV—Got Anger?
7. The Phone Call 61
8. The Valentine Blues 65
9. The Matchmakers 71

Section V—Resting in the Lord
10. The Dating Game 79
11. How Do You Know If You Have Found the Right One? 85
12. Leave Loneliness Alone 93

Section VI—Are You in Your Garden?
13. Being in the Right Place at the Right Time 105
14. Passion and Purity 111
15. Secret Petitions 119

Section VII—Forgiveness, Freedom, and Healing

16. Is That You, God? 127
17. Look in the Mirror; What Do You See? 131

Section VIII—Single Again

18. I Thought for Sure I'd Never Be Single *Again* 139

Section IX—Final Thoughts

19. A Little Friendly Advice 151

Section X—Scriptural Prayers

20. Thank-You Prayers 161
    Why Am I Still Single? *163*
    When Is It Going to Be My Turn? *165*
    HELP! My Best Friend Is Getting Married *167*
    I Thought for Sure I'd Never be Single Again *168*
    Wisdom and Discernment *171*
    Insecurities and a Lack of Confidence *176*
    I Just Got Dumped *178*
    Healing from the Past *183*
    The Unknown Future *186*
    Purity *189*
    Depression *191*
    Loneliness *194*
    Discouragement *195*
    Receiving Forgiveness *196*
    Giving Forgiveness *199*
    Your Future Mate *200*
    Closing Prayer *201*

Acknowledgements

A sincere thank you to the following contributing editors: Barbara Robidoux, Beth McLendon, and Jennifer Morris.

My deepest appreciation to...

Scott Kays—It was the testimony of your book getting published that initially motivated me to go forward and begin to pursue my vision to write books. Also, your words of encouragement and your excitement for writing played a big role in helping me complete this project.

Brad Thompson—you helped me more than you realize. It is a special person who can know you briefly, but still help you greatly.

Robin Gant—you were there helping me before the word book was in my mouth. Thank you for editing all those articles, many of which I used to write this book.

Cecil Murphy—Your sincere love for God and your pure motives for writing were always refreshing. No matter how busy you were writing books of your own, you always dropped what you were doing and gave this rookie advice. You never made me feel insignificant.

My ultimate thanks and appreciation goes to God. As You know, this book is a product of Your grace. You enabled me to do what my mind thought impossible for so many years.

Introduction

So, you thought for sure you would be married by now! There are thousands of singles who have thought the same thing—"I'm *still* on the journey to marriage?" A single person's journey to marriage is one of life's most significant journeys. Webster defines *journey* as "a traveling from one place to another." Life is made up of all kinds of journeys. What's important to know is that a successful journey is not about crossing the finish line as much as making the most of every step.

All life's journeys have their pros and cons, joys and discouragements. Most journeys share some common challenges, such as needing patience, overcoming obstacles, and being tempted to focus on negative attributes. However, the single's journey to marriage possesses its own unique set of circumstances, especially when a person has crossed the age of when he or she thought the journey would be over.

A danger for a single person is to think that life only starts at marriage, that you're not "complete" until you find your "better half." We know this is not true. But when someone meditates on something, even when it is untrue, it can cause emotional despair and anxiety.

The single's life is too often riddled with loneliness, worry, fear, frustration, anger, discouragement, and a host of other emotions. But the truth is, it doesn't have to be that way. I believe a person can learn to overcome any challenge of a particular journey and enjoy a peace-filled trip.

For many years I struggled with the challenges most unmarried people face: *Why am I still single? Will I ever find the right one? What's wrong with me?* And of course, *I thought for sure I'd be married by now!* In my search for answers to these questions and other challenges, I discovered principles on how to turn worry and frustration into peace. As I applied God's wisdom, He saw me through my times of frustration, discouragement, and loneliness.

This book will share those principles with you. Although my goal is to minister to singles, these are not merely keys for single people. Nor are they keys that automatically open the doors to marriage. What you will discover are keys that will enable you to enjoy where you are, on the way to where you are going—in any area of life.

Discussion Questions

I strongly encourage you to find a few friends to join you in reading this book. At the end of each section, you will notice discussion questions designed to help you grow. Consider meeting once a week to discuss each section. Reading and discussing a book with a friend or group of friends provides many added benefits. A small group creates the opportunity to learn from others as you share your own life's experiences. You can also minister to each other with prayer and encouragement.

Let this book be a way for you to get to know other singles and possibly develop meaningful relationships. Ecclesiastes 4:9 and 12 says, "Two are better than one, because they have a good reward for their labor. Though one may be overpowered by another, two can withstand him. And a threefold cord is not quickly broken."

Any journey is better with friends!

Psalm 37:1-8, 23-24

Do not fret because of evildoers,
Be not envious toward wrongdoers.
For they will wither quickly like the grass,
And fade like the green herb.
Trust in the Lord, and do good;
Dwell in the land and cultivate faithfulness.
Delight yourself in the Lord;
And He will give you the desires of your heart.
Commit your way to the Lord,
Trust also in Him, and He will do it.
And He will bring forth your righteousness as the light,
And your judgment as the noonday.

Rest in the Lord and wait patiently for Him;
Do not fret because of him who prospers in his way,
Because of the man who carries out wicked schemes.
Cease from anger, and forsake wrath;
Do not fret, it leads only to evildoing.

The steps of a man are established by the Lord;
And He delights in his way.
When he falls, he shall not be hurled headlong;
Because the Lord is the One who holds his hand.

(NAS)

Section I
The Big Picture

Chapter One

Are We There Yet?

*"Life is not about crossing finish lines as much
as it is about running the race and becoming a better runner!"*

Life is full of journeys, small and large, from driving to work to accomplishing your life's vision. Recently my wife Pippa and I took our two small children on a trip to Florida. Throughout the five-hour drive, we heard the all too familiar words echoing from the back seat. "Are we there yet?"

To which we kept responding, "Not yet."

"How much longer? When are we going to get there?"

The stereo effect of my daughters behind my head was resounding. The more they asked, the longer the trip seemed. After a few hours of driving, the children were weary of hearing, "Not yet" and "It won't be long." Finally, in an effort to put an end to the asking, I resorted to answering like I remembered my father answering. "We will get there when we get there! Sit back and enjoy the trip!"

For a while, the children stopped asking, "Are we there yet?" Time passed quickly. Everyone enjoyed playing games and eating snacks. Before the children knew it, we had entered Florida.

The more you ask, "Are we there yet?" the longer the trip will seem. Why? Because your focus is on the unmet desire instead of enjoying the trip. Asking if you're there only serves to remind you that you are not there yet.

Kids! When will they ever learn to stop asking, "Are we there yet?" and just sit back and enjoy the trip? Probably when adults stop asking God the same question. What do I mean, you ask. How many times have you asked God, "Are we there yet?" when it comes to your own journeys to desired destinations? "When am I going to get my own car?" "When is my boss ever going to promote me?" Maybe it's your journey from renting an apartment to becoming a homeowner. For many singles it is the journey to marriage. "When am I ever going to get married? I thought for sure I'd be married by now!"

But wait, the question of, "Are we there yet?" doesn't stop at marriage. For many couples, after a few months of trying to have a baby, the "Are we there yet?" question becomes, "When are we ever going to be pregnant?"

I call it "the sin of when," and it starts early in life. When I get my driver's license, then I will be happy. Then you get your license and find out Mom makes you drive your little sister around all the time. Then it is, When I graduate and go to college, then I will be happy. College isn't the cakewalk of party freedom you thought it was going to be, and you then think, When I get into my career and make a lot of money, then I will be happy. You graduate and get a job. Welcome to the real world of paying bills and dealing with a boss and coworkers. Now you want to be married. When I get married, then I will be happy. You get married and now want kids. Junior and little Sis arrive and then I've heard people say, When these kids leave home, then we'll be happy. They leave you alone with your spouse of twenty years and you look at each other and say, "When are our children going to give us some grandchildren?"

Listen friend, when never gets here!

The fact is, we are on multiple journeys throughout life. We cross one finish line only to find more desires, races yet to run. And, no matter how old we get, we tend to ask, "Are we there yet?"

In a moment we will focus on the single's journey to marriage. But first, let's put things into perspective and look at the journey everyone is on, regardless of their marital status. It's the journey of your high calling to become like Christ and fulfill your God-given purpose—from discovering to actually walking in your God-ordained destiny.

Like you, I am on this journey to Christ-likeness and fulfilling my specific God-given purpose in life. I know my final calling in life is to pastor a church with a ministry school that propels people into full-time ministry. Do I have a church yet? No. Do I have a ministry school yet? No. Is that dream even close to happening? I don't know, but it doesn't look like it. Have I asked God, "Are we there yet?" Yes, many times over the years. In fact, I have done what everyone else has done. At times, I have allowed the unmet desire of walking in my final calling to dictate my present emotional state. Then God taught me the principles you are about to learn in this book.

I have learned the danger of always asking "Are we there yet?" I have determined that even if I am eighty years old and have not yet realized my dream of having a church, it will make no difference as to how I live my life now. The key is to not allow my future desire to rob me of my present peace and joy. Instead, I've learned to release the unmet desire to the Lord and trust Him to orchestrate His plan.

After all, a Christian's ultimate goal in life is not to fulfill a dream but to become like Christ. Desires and goals, like getting promoted, getting married, having kids, walking in your destiny, are all secondary to what should be the ultimate goal of every

Christian, to become like Christ and fulfill our ministry of reconciliation (2 Corinthians 5:18). In fact, God uses journeys to form and fashion us into His image.

It dawned on me during our journey to Florida that the trip was not only about getting somewhere, it was actually serving as a tool in God's hands to develop His purposes in our lives. The children were learning patience along with their dad. God was binding us closer as a family. A strength was being developed in us. God's character qualities, like patience, humility, love, and the other fruit of the Spirit would never be produced if we always got what we wanted when we wanted it.

God's Word talks about an athlete who runs a race to obtain a corruptible crown, but we Christians run the race to receive an incorruptible prize.

> And everyone who competes for the prize is temperate in all things. Now they do it to obtain a perishable crown, but we for an imperishable crown. (1 Corinthians 9:25-26)

This verse is talking about the big race of life in general, but it also includes the smaller races every one of us runs each day.

The perishable crown represents earthly desires: promotion, house, marriage, children, etc. The imperishable crown first represents eternal salvation, but doesn't stop there. The imperishable crown, the one worth attaining, is developing the unseen attributes of Christ, attained by running the race righteously. The inward crown of strength, courage, patience, character, integrity, and humility are all crowns to be desired above simply crossing a finish line. These crowns should be our higher goal during any and all journeys, including the single's journey to marriage.

Keep this perspective as you read the following chapters. It will help you learn to enjoy the journey and not to allow your present circumstances get you down. Always remember, marriage is not the crown that you are ultimately after. Marriage will probably come, but the character you build while on the journey—that is the crown you want to attain!

What joy or true fulfillment is there in crossing a finish line if you're the same person you were when you started running? Joy at the finish comes by receiving the greater prize of developing Christ-like character on the way.

It is not married people who live a fulfilled life, doing significant things for God. *Fulfilled* people doing significant things for God are those living a life of surrender, allowing the character of Jesus to shine through for the world to see.

So you get married…whoopee do. The real journey, the journey of all journeys that every Believer is on, is the journey to Christ-likeness. A godly marriage, godly children, fulfilling godly dreams, are all by-products of becoming like Christ.

That's the big picture. It applies to everyone; but there are specific issues of a single's journey to possible marriage that need to be addressed and I trust your life will never be the same as you read.

Where do you start? You start by releasing the desire for marriage to God and putting it in His hands to orchestrate. Maintaining this *big-picture* perspective will help you release your future dreams to the Lord and find peace and fulfillment in the journey.

After many years of being single, and crossing the age that I thought I would be married, I finally got to that point of release with my desire for marriage. This book will help you get there, too. The point is, we need to stop allowing an unreached finish line to discourage us from pressing on and attaining imperishable crowns. Life is not about crossing finish lines as much as it is about running the race and becoming a better runner!

Marriage is seen as such a major accomplishment that a single person's thought of their wedding is coupled with a big sigh of relief. "*Whew*, I made it! I am so glad that journey is over." But there are even more significant journeys ahead, such as staying married to your mate in purity and love, growing a family, the responsibility of raising godly children in this dark world to one day launch them into society to do more significant things than yourself. And always there is the ever-important journey of finding and fulfilling your God-given purpose in life. (If you haven't heard, your purpose in life is not to get married. Your purpose in life is to become like Christ, discover what God created you for, and fulfill that specific calling.)

The next time you are tempted to ask God, "Are we there yet?" remember what my father told me when I was a kid: "We will get there when we get there. Just sit back and enjoy the trip."

Although you can find a book for practically every aspect in life, this one focuses on helping singles on their journey to marriage. In the chapters ahead, we will focus on the single's journey leading to possible marriage with an emphasis on not allowing the desire for marriage, or other future desires, to rob your present joy and blind you to your ultimate goals of becoming like Christ and fulfilling His purpose for your life.

The single's life can be full of mental battles over marital status and unmet desires. Valentine's Day with no valentine is tough. Then there's the whole dating scene—is it really possible to believe people when they tell you, "You'll just know when the right person comes along"? Worse yet, how do you handle your best friend's engagement to Mr. Tall-dark-and-handsome, while all you get are calls from matchmakers who set you up with friends who have "great personalities"?

I learned a lot during my single years. I was a dedicated Christian, living a fulfilled life as an associate minister. However, mixed in with seasons of joy and happiness were times of discouragement and frustration. The more I pondered my marital status and focused on the seemingly happy couples around me, the less I seemed to enjoy life. I had a particularly difficult time when I would see an immoral couple enjoying life to its fullest.

My flesh would cry out, "It's not fair! When am I ever going to get married? How come I'm not there yet?"

I trust the truths in the following chapters will help you sit back and enjoy the trip. When you apply God's Word, it *is* possible to enjoy where you are on the way to where you are going.

DISCUSSION QUESTIONS

1. Do you desire to be married one day? Do you consider yourself on the journey to marriage?

2. Have you ever asked the question, "Are we there yet?" when thinking about your desire to be married?

3. What other journeys are you on?

4. What are some of the most difficult challenges of being single?

Section II
Don't Worry; Be Happy!

CHAPTER TWO

Do Not Fret

*"Do not fret because of evildoers,
Be not envious toward wrongdoers."*
PSALM 37:1 (NAS)

Bill could vaguely hear what the fight was about in the apartment next door. "Why can't things be like they used to be?" the man yelled. "Why do you have to talk to him all the time and invite him over here?"

"Just leave me alone," the woman screamed back. "I should be able to talk to anyone I want. You don't own me!"

Then Bill heard a big crash, like something had been thrown against a wall. What was going on over there? Bill was twenty-seven and had been living in that single apartment for about two years. He barely knew the young couple next door, but was moved with compassion to go over and see if anyone was hurt. When Bill knocked on the door, the yelling stopped, and he heard whispering.

"Who is it?" a timid voice asked.

"It's your neighbor, Bill. Is everything okay?"

Sheri slowly opened the door a crack, keeping the safety chain hitched. Bill could see enough of the apartment to know that they'd just had a knock-down, drag-out fight.

"Is Todd hurting you?" Bill asked.

"No," she answered.

Then Todd opened the door wide and announced, "If anyone is getting hurt, it's me."

It was obvious to Bill that he was telling the truth. Todd's forehead was bleeding and a broken table leaf lay on the floor, five feet from the dining-room table. Bill made his way into the apartment, carefully stepped over the broken leaf, and scanned the scene. Water was boiling on the stove. Chairs were overturned, and what looked like dinner dripped from the wall that connected their apartments. Todd and Sheri were perspiring and both were trying to catch their breath as if they had just sprinted the 200-meter dash. Bill's presence calmed the violent storm.

Bill's neighbors were barely twenty and supposedly engaged. Just last week, they had told Bill how they were so happily in love. The devil actually used this declaration to discourage Bill, because it pointed out something he did not have—a true love relationship. *Why do they get to have so much fun?* Bill thought at the time. *It's not fair.* When a single person sees a happy couple, it's difficult not to entertain thoughts of fear and discouragement. Bill thought for sure he would have been married by now and was left with one painful question: *Am I ever going to have somebody to enjoy life with?*

It was difficult for Bill to sit alone hearing laughter coming from the apartment next door. At such times, the devil whispered things like, "If you weren't such a goody-two-shoes, maybe you could have as much fun as they are having. You'll never have any fun if you keep this serious Christian thing going. You'll always be alone."

As Bill stood in Todd and Sheri's living room that day, he realized their happiness was shallow. The couple who appeared to be in a state of eternal bliss were living an empty lie. There are many couples like Todd and Sheri who appear happy, but when the dust settles, literally in some cases, the truth of their emptiness is painfully revealed. Sheri eventually moved out, and Bill barely saw Todd again. Todd and Sheri had been together for a whole five months.

When Bill returned to his apartment after his Good Samaritan rescue, he smelt smoke coming from his kitchen. The frozen pizza he had put in the oven before the battle of the sexes broke out was now burnt to a crisp. So much for heroic rescues and being a peacemaker!

Have you ever been the Good Samaritan only to return to burnt pizza? It's amazing how God always shows up to comfort us. By His grace, He uses challenging times to draw us closer to Him in a special way. God seems to always try to get us into thanksgiving in order to get us off a pity track and back on Him. Even though you cannot see or touch God, you can always take a deep breath and go on knowing He is with you.

Psalm 37 gives us tremendous insights into living a victorious life as a Believer. In it, the psalmist, David, addresses the issue of dealing with wrongdoers and their appearance of success.

> Do not fret because of evildoers, be not envious toward wrongdoers. For they will wither quickly like the grass, and fade like the green herb. (Psalm 37:1-2 NAS)

Let's look at how this passage directly relates to the single person. The word *fret* encompasses a wide range of emotions including anger, worry, jealousy, and stress. The *wrongdoer* in this verse can represent those who live their lives according to the world's standards. Such are people like Todd and Sheri who live with little to no regard for righteousness or God's ways.

What the verse is telling us is: Don't get stressed out when you see people doing things the world's way. Don't get anxious or worried when you see your peers throwing conviction to the wind and living after the dictates of the flesh, thus seeming to have all the fun. Don't get jealous when you hear that two people are moving in together because they are "so much in love." "For they *[and their happiness]* will wither quickly like the grass, and fade like the green herb." (Psalm 37:2 NAS)

A biblical principle says that anyone who defies wisdom and chooses the wrong way will have short-lived pleasure and success. That's a good enough reason right there for you to listen to wisdom and choose to live your life according to God's Word. Who wants to wither? It is also a reason for you not to envy the wrongdoer, since his or her way will have a bitter end.

Another reason we need to stay away from fret and worry is found in the latter portion of Psalm 37:8 (NAS). It says, "Do not fret, *it leads* only to evildoing." Whenever we allow ourselves to enter into worry or fear, we tend to start doing things the wrong way. For example, let's look at Susie. She's a twenty-eight-year-old single woman with high Christian standards. Susie dresses modestly and does not enter into flirting. However, she notices that all the men look at Jennifer every time she enters a room. Jennifer's blouses are semi-sheer and low cut. The slit in her skirt reaches her mid thigh and she struts like a supermodel.

Susie watches the men *oohing* and *ahhing* and falling all over Jennifer. She begins to think, "It sure would be nice to get some of that attention." Then she frets, "If I don't do something, I could be single all my life. No one looks at me like they look at her. Maybe if I were to unbutton my top button and wear a shorter skirt then they might notice me. Perhaps if I wore more perfume and walked shaking my hips a little more, I might attract a man." Susie's fear tempts her to enter wrongdoing.

Psalm 37 teaches us not to enter into such fear. The key is not to fret when you see people living according to the world's standards, enjoying unholy dating relationships, and even getting married. However, I agree that's a whole lot easier said than done: "Go ye and fret not. Amen!"

Would you like to know how to stay out of stress and live in peace regardless of what people are doing around you? Would you like to learn how to overcome anger, fear, and a host of other adverse emotions regardless of your circumstances? The answer is in Philippians 4:6-7. I call it the secret of turning worry into peace through Thank-You Prayers.

Chapter Three

The Power of Thank-You Prayers

"Be anxious for nothing, but in everything by prayer and supplication, with thanksgiving, let your requests be made known to God."
Philippians 4:6

I'm often asked how I handled my single years before marrying at age thirty.

Here's how: I prayed a lot. It wasn't that I sat down and prayed for two hours a day; I prayed *throughout* the day. Prayer is simply communicating with God. But the kind of prayer I'm referring to is a special kind of prayer mentioned in Philippians 4:6. The verse begins with the same phrase as Psalm 37:1.

> Do not fret *or* have any anxiety about anything, but in every circumstance *and* in everything, by prayer and petition (definite requests), with thanksgiving, continue to make your wants known to God. (AMP)

Instead of getting anxious, pray. Paul even tells us what kind of prayer. He says pray *with thanksgiving*. Notice, however, that he does not stop there but commands that we, "continue to make your wants known to God." Paul is describing a type of prayer we can practice on a daily basis. Thank-You Prayers are simple, but one of the Bible's most powerful keys to a fulfilled life.

When it hurts to hear that a friend is getting engaged, don't get stressed, pray: "Thank You, Jesus, that one day I'll be able to announce my engagement." When you are hurt by another person, pray: "Thank You, Jesus, for being the healer of the brokenhearted." Coming home to an empty apartment, watching people kiss, attending wedding celebrations alone—all are situations prayer can help you through.

In every situation, you have a choice. Are you going to meditate on the negatives and get more depressed and frustrated, or are you going to turn the situation into a Thank-You Prayer and allow the peace of God to flow into your heart?

Developing the habit of facing every situation with Thank-You Prayers will change your life! But the best part is yet to come. If we do what verse 6 says, we get the promise found in verse 7:

> And God's peace [shall be yours, that tranquil state of soul assured of its salvation through Christ, and so fearing nothing from God and being content with its earthly lot of whatever sort that is, that peace] which transcends all understanding shall garrison *and* mount guard over your hearts and minds in Christ Jesus. (Philippians 4:7 AMP)

If we turn worry into prayer with thanksgiving, God's peace mounts guard over our hearts and minds. That's exactly what we need in stressful times. We need God's peace!

Let's look at this Scripture more closely. It says, "The peace of God will mount guard over your hearts and minds in Christ Jesus." Some translations say "through" Christ Jesus. The words translated *in* and *through* come from the same Greek word—*en*. According to *Strong's Concordance*, the word *en* is a primary preposition denoting fixed position. In other words, the word *en* means to be fixed positionally on someone or something. For example, the other day there was a gorgeous sunset. I stopped what I was doing, turned my head to the west, and *fixed my eyes on* the beauty of the sun setting over the horizon.

With this definition in mind, let's look at the verse in the King James Version.

> Be careful for nothing; but in everything by prayer and supplication with thanksgiving let your requests be made known unto God. And the peace of God, which passeth all understanding, shall keep your hearts and minds through *[fixed positionally on]* Christ Jesus. (Philippians 4:6 KJV)

Practicing the kind of prayer Paul teaches in verse 6 causes our hearts to be fixed on Christ in a state of peace. Thank-You Prayers get our minds off the source of stress and onto the Source of peace. "Be careful for nothing" is another way of saying not to get stressed out, anxious, frustrated, or fearful. The original definition of the phrase *be careful* indicates that the stress is coming as a result of a distraction. So instead of letting a situation distract you from Christ, causing stress, pray with thanksgiving and let God know your request. Then the peace of God will come and keep your hearts and minds fixed positionally on Jesus. When our hearts and minds are on Jesus, we are full of peace, as confirmed by Isaiah 26:3: "You will keep *him* in perfect peace, *Whose* mind *is* stayed *on You*, Because he trusts in You."

When we allow situations to distract us and get our eyes off God, our hearts are open to fear and worry. But if we can keep our minds stayed on the Lord, our hearts will remain open to His peace. The key is keeping our mind on Jesus. So how do we do this? We do Philippians 4:6: "Do not fret *or* have any anxiety about anything, but in every circumstance *and* in everything, by prayer and petition (definite requests), with thanksgiving, continue to make your wants known to God. (AMP)

How do you overcome challenges of singleness? A great way is by practicing Thank-You Prayers, and not just one Thank-You Prayer in the morning, but throughout the day. Let's say you're walking down the street and the thought comes, "I'm never going to get married." That's a situation. Turn it into a Thank-You Prayer and let God know your desire: "Thank You, Jesus, that my future is in Your hands."

Situation: "No one will ever love me. I've made too many mistakes."

What is your response? "Thank You, God, that I am free from my past. It is behind me and under the blood of Jesus. Because of You, there is someone special who truly loves me more than anything in the world."

At night, when you lay your head on your pillow, you hear laughter coming from the couple next door, and a sense of loneliness tries to creep into your heart. You pray, "Thank You, Jesus, I know You are right here with me. You never leave me alone."

Whenever a thought of discouragement knocks on the door of your mind, turn it into a Thank-You Prayer and let God know your desire. You may be in the grocery store, stopped at a red light, at the movies, a high school reunion, or eating in a restaurant—Thank-You Prayers will always help you turn your heart toward God and experience His peace.

How Many Times?

So, how many times do you need to say a Thank-You Prayer? As many times as stress or anxiety knock at the door of your mind. It could be fifty times in a day, but only five times on another day. The principle takes practice to keep your heart and mind constantly fixed on God. At first, you might allow your heart to be troubled before thinking of uttering a Thank-You Prayer. Then the Holy Spirit will remind you of the principle and you will have the choice to apply it or not. Once you begin to apply the principle and practice Thank-You Prayers, it will soon become a habit.

In fact, you can let the devil remind you to pray. When the devil tells you, "You will never get married," tell him this: "Thank you, devil, for reminding me to pray. Father, thank You for bringing me the desires of my heart."

The devil drops this thought into your mind, "You are a loser. No one will ever love you."

You say, "Thanks for the reminder. Thank You, Jesus, that the same Spirit that raised Christ from the dead dwells within me and with You, I am a winner!" Eventually, you will learn to turn any attack of fear and worry into thanksgiving.

This principle found in Philippians holds true in every area of life, not just when a person is frustrated with his or her marital status. You may be waiting for a new job or a promotion and the devil will say, "You'll never get it. You're not good enough. You'll never be able to get ahead financially." If that happens, you can choose to focus your attention on the problem, or you can turn that worry into peace-gaining prayer.

> Father, thank You for giving me the wisdom to earn a promotion. I thank You that I have divine favor and You go before me preparing the way. I trust in You, Lord. In Jesus' name, amen.

Thank-You Prayers help in any situation—stress, worry, frustration, anxiety, anger, hurt, mistakes, discouragement, dismay, hopelessness, fear, doubt, jealousy, temptation, and anything else the devil throws your way.

"But, Brother Jeff, I tried Thank-You Prayers and they didn't change my circumstances," you say. That's true. Thank-You Prayers don't change circumstances. But I've got news for you—

complaining and getting stressed out won't change circumstances either. But God's peace in the middle of a difficult time is far better than being filled with frustration. Thank-You Prayers may not change the situation, but they will change you and your emotions by opening the gates for God's peace.

This book is not designed to change your circumstances or your marital status. My vision is to teach you how to have peace and fulfillment regardless of life situations. Trying to alter your circumstances through your own ability usually causes more frustration. When you learn to have peace, you will enjoy life more and be in a position to receive God's wisdom.

I remember one of the first times I was invited to preach in a church in a town near my home in Rockford, Illinois. (To be honest, in those days I probably wasn't invited. I more than likely begged the pastor to let me preach!) I was single and in my early twenties. On my way to the church, I got lost. Well, being a guy, technically I was not lost. I just couldn't find the church. Anyway, I began to get nervous. I had given myself plenty of time to get there, but time was running out. I finally swallowed my manly pride and stopped to ask for directions. (Sorry guys.) A lot of good that did, the guy in the MiniMart never heard of the church.

I began to perspire. *What am I going to do? I'm the guest speaker and I'm going to be late. Worse yet, I might miss the meeting altogether.* Then it dawned on me. *Use the pay phone and call the church.* Great idea! I called and the answering machine picked up. "Hello, thank you for calling . . ."

By this time, I felt like shouting, "HELP! I'm lost! Pick up the doggone phone."

I quickly ran back to the car. Oh, yeah, I forgot to tell you it was raining cats and dogs—another added pleasure to the whole experience. I sat there utterly in despair. "I can't believe this. Why did You let this happen, God?" I wailed. "I'm on my way to do Your good business and this happens?"

Then a small inner voice softly said, "Why don't you thank Me and give Me praise?" My first reaction was, "Ah, God, I don't have time to praise You right now. I'm late!" Again the still, small voice. "Why don't you thank and praise Me?"

"I'll praise You when I get there!" I thought.

But, by His grace, I slowly began to obey. "Well, okay God," I said halfheartedly, while glancing at my watch. "I thank You. I praise You." *I have five minutes, God.* "I thank You, I praise You." *Nothing is happening, God.* Finally I decided to forget what was going on and really start thanking Him and letting Him know my desires.

> Lord, I thank You for all You are doing in my life. Thank You for this opportunity to serve You and preach Your Word. Thank You for helping me find the church. I praise You for who You are—the King of kings and Lord of lords.

At that point, I was carefree. "I don't care if I ever make it to the church; I'm just enjoying giving God praise." My situation had not changed—I was still lost—but, as I turned my attention to the Lord, peace began to slowly fill my heart and drive out the stress. Thank-You Prayers quieted my mind and put me in a position to hear the soft whispers of the Lord.

In the midst of this increasing peace, I sensed the Lord saying, "Get back on the main road going east." I remember thinking, "I don't think that's right, but I'll try it anyway." I drove down the road continuing in thanksgiving. The inner voice said, "You see that traffic light? Turn left there." "Now, I know that's wrong," I thought. "But what do I have to lose?" I turned left at the light, looked up, and the church was right there. I could not believe it! I made it into the building just before the service started and, of course, pretended like nothing had happened.

That's not the end of the story. The title of my message that evening was "The Power of Praise and Thanksgiving." I was actually going to preach on how Thank-You Prayers and praise can help you live free from stress. The Lord sure has a sense of humor! When I stood to preach, He told me to use what had just happened to me as an example. I obeyed, with some reservations, and the people were ministered to in a great way. Thank You, Jesus!

I have told this story for two reasons. First, to illustrate that the principle of Thank-You Prayers is useful in every area of life, and second, to emphasize the need for practice. Even though I had been using this principle in my own life and was even on my way to teach on the subject, it was obvious I needed to improve my application.

All of us get distracted at times and allow our hearts to get stressed. That's okay. We are on a journey toward complete maturity in the Lord. Remember, the more you practice the principle of Thank-You Prayers, the less you will experience anxiety and the more you will enjoy the journeys of life. I know I have a long way to go, but I also know I have made a lot of progress. You will be able to say the same thing after you apply this secret of enjoyment in your life.

Chapter Four

A Typical Day's Journey

"Therefore we do not lose heart. Though outwardly we are wasting away, yet inwardly we are being renewed day by day. For our light and momentary troubles are achieving for us an eternal glory that far outweighs them all."
2 Corinthians 4:16-17 (NIV)

One day a six-year-old boy told his mom that he knew that God's name was Andy. When asked how he knew such information, he responded confidently, "Because that is what the song says: 'Andy walks with me; Andy talks with me.'" Whether His name is Andy or not, we know that God desires to walk with us every moment of every day. Here is a sample of how that can be done:

6:00 a.m.—As your feet hit the floor, the devil whispers in your ear, "This is going to be a bad day."

Thank You, Jesus, that this is the day You have made. I choose to rejoice and be glad in it.

6:30 a.m.—You're in the shower and you hear, "Don't forget to send a wedding card to your younger sister, Jeanne. By the way, you're never going to get married."

> Thank You, Jesus, that my life is in Your hands and You will bring me a mate in Your timing.

7:00 a.m.—You're eating breakfast and you wonder what kind of cereal your future mate will prefer. Then the devil says, "Don't hold your breath. You're going to be single for a long time. In fact, you may never get married."

> Thank You, Jesus, because Your Word says You will give me the desires of my heart. I delight myself in You now and thank You for always being with me.

7:30 a.m.—You're driving to work and you hear a radio ad for a marriage enrichment seminar. It hits you again: "I can't believe I'm still single. I should be going to marriage conferences, not singles conferences."

> Thank You, Jesus, I am content in You. Thank You that I am complete in You and I don't have to be married to be fulfilled. Thank You for teaching me how to be a good mate now so I can be the best for my future spouse.

8:00 a.m.—You arrive at work. Your boss drops a stack of work on your desk and tells you to be done before you leave today. Stress rises, coupled with frustration.

> Thank You, Jesus, I can do all things through You. Thank You I have the mind of

Christ and You are giving me the wisdom to accomplish this task. I work as unto You and look to You for my reward.

12:00 noon—You're eating lunch and your coworkers are swapping dirty jokes. When they see you, they start making goody-two-shoes remarks. You are tempted to snap back, but instead you turn your anger into prayer.

Thank You, Jesus, for giving me the strength to overcome evil with good. I bless these people and I ask You to draw them to repentance by Your love.

5:00 p.m.—You are driving home through traffic and a bozo cuts in front of you, practically running you off the road. You want to catch up to him and ride his tail all the way home. You sense your blood starting to boil.

Thank You, Jesus, for keeping me safe. Thank You for giving me grace to keep my peace.

6:00 p.m.—You stop at the store to get a precooked meal for tonight's dinner. The parking lot is packed; it's raining, and you don't have an umbrella.

Father, thank You for giving me a close parking place. Thank You for divine favor. Even if I have to park far away, that's all right. I'm not going to let a little rain get me down.

6:05 p.m.—You see a parking place close to the front and head straight for it. Right when you get there, a teenager pulls in before you with a cocky grin a mile long. You take a deep breath and say,

> Thank You, Jesus, for giving me the grace to say, "Thank You, Jesus!" Lord, I refuse to get frustrated so I thank You for another close parking spot.

6:07 p.m.— You find a closer parking place.

> Thank You, Jesus, for looking out for me.

6:45 P.M.—You are on your way home, looking forward to relaxing on your couch, and you get stopped by a red light. In the car in front of you sits a couple gazing into each other's eyes in a state of bliss. You try to ignore them, but you can't. The devil floods your mind with frustration and anxiety. *I'm a loser,* you tell yourself. *Look at them having so much fun. They're probably newlyweds—something I'll never be.* You feel a little overwhelmed and caught off guard.

> Thank You, Jesus, for comforting me now and helping me keep my eyes on You. I release the whole idea of marriage to You and thank You that my future is in Your hands.

7:00 p.m.—You arrive home to an empty apartment and a sense of loneliness tries to settle in.

> Thank You, Jesus, that I'm never alone because You are right here with me. Thank You for giving me an idea of what to do tonight to overcome this lonely feeling.

7:05 p.m.—You call and invite a good friend over for dinner. "Pick up a movie on the way," you tell him.

7:35 p.m.—You are enjoying the meal when your friend leans over with a smile on his face and says he has an announcement to make. You brace yourself and secretly beg God for mercy. Please God, don't let him say that he's engaged. "I got a promotion today!" Whew, you let out a huge sigh of relief and congratulate him. "Yeah, and it could not have come at a better time. I asked Jessica to marry me today and she said, 'Yes.' The date is set for February 14th!"

"What? You're getting married?" Under your breath you pray,

> Thank You, Jesus, for the day I can announce my own wedding plans. Thank You for helping me trust You to do what only You know is best for me in the meantime. Father, bless my friend and his engagement.

7:50 p.m.—Your friend says he has to go. He wants to make the announcement in person to several other friends. "Bye, and congratulations again," you say as you close the door a little firmer than usual. The thought comes: I thought for sure I'd be married by now. When is it going to be my turn?

> Lord, thank You that my future rests in Your hands. Thank You for manifesting Your love and comfort in my life right now. Thank You for giving me the grace to wait on You.

8:00 p.m.—You're watching the movie. You look around and loneliness tries to creep in again.

> Thank You, Jesus, that I have more than one friend.

8:15 p.m.—You call a few friends and find a couple who are free for coffee. As you drive to the restaurant, a sense of peace fills your heart. It's as if Jesus Himself is sitting in the passenger seat next to you. You can't explain it, but you know everything is going to be okay.

> Thank You, Jesus, for Your presence. Thank You for filling me with Your peace and confidence.

10:30 p.m.—You get ready for bed and again you are reminded that you are alone.

> Thank You, Jesus, for being with me at all times.

11:00 p.m.—You're lying in bed and you whisper,

> I love You, Jesus. Thank You for a good night's sleep and for my waking in the morning refreshed and ready to tackle another day with You.

I know this may not be a typical day for you, but it gives you an idea of how you can pray Thank-You Prayers throughout the day to maintain peace in your life. In the following chapters, you will read how Thank-You Prayers have helped me, and how they can play a major role in helping you get through difficult challenges. As you read, make the commitment to practice Thank-You Prayers in your own life.

Discussion Questions

1. What do you need to do when faced with anxious circumstances?

2. Are there any circumstances in your life, specifically related to being single, that cause you to fret? Write down and discuss some specific thoughts that the devil uses to get you worried, angry, depressed, or frustrated.

3. Take your list in question 2, and discuss how you can turn each of them into a Thank-You Prayer. Then write the prayers down.

For example:

> **Thought:** Sometimes I think that I don't deserve a good future because of my miserable past.
> **Prayer:** Thank You, Jesus, that You have redeemed me from my past and because of You, I have a bright future.

Your turn:

4. If you are part of a small group reading this book together, make a commitment to help remind each other to practice Thank-You Prayers. If you're not in a small group...start one!

Section III
Trusting God

Chapter Five

You're in Good Hands

"Trust in the LORD, and do good; Dwell in the land and cultivate faithfulness. Trust also in Him, and He will do it."
Psalm 37:3,5b (NAS)

Jamie glanced over her shoulder with a puzzled look as she clenched the ladder with all her might. A group of her friends were standing under the ladder with their hands and arms linked. "Just let go," they shouted. "Don't worry; we'll catch you."

Have you ever participated in this exercise? The instructor was attempting to demonstrate the concept of trust. Trust is putting your faith in someone other than yourself. How many times have we been told to "let go and let God"? Let's be honest; neither is easy to do. Most people don't want to *let go* of their control and many don't want to *let God*. This may be why I believe trusting God is one of the most powerful actions of a Believer.

Psalm 37 tells us to trust in the Lord in verse 3 right after it says "fret not" in verse 1. So let's see what happens when we link verses 1 and 3 together with the word *instead*. When we do, we get "Fret not because of evil doers, instead, trust in the Lord." Trust is actually the opposite of fear. Trust is what we fall back on in every area of our life and what our Christian faith is based on. We trust that our bodies will perform as expected, that our relationships will stand the test of time, and that the Bible is true and God is faithful. Such fundamental trusting needs to include our thoughts for the future.

So, how do we let go and trust God? The same way we let go of stress and seize peace. We get our eyes off the circumstance and onto Jesus through Thank-You Prayers. I can't tell you how many times I have said:

> Thank You, God, that I can trust You with my future. I trust You, Lord, and know that You will take care of me.

Verse 5 of Psalm 37 also speaks of trust: "Trust also in Him and He will do it." Do what? Whatever you are trusting Him for according to His will. If you trust God, He will bring your desire to pass. On the other hand, if you do not trust God, He will not do it. The choice is yours.

Trust is not a simple term to define. However, I know that trusting God does not mean sitting at home watching television all day until He brings a gorgeous woman or handsome man to your door. Even though with God all things are possible, that is not a likely scenario. Some people use the concept of trust and rest as an excuse to do nothing for themselves. Instead of joining a club or going to meetings, they become downright introverted. But trust does not mean you should sit in your living room lit with candles and hum, "I trust You, Lord. You will do it, Lord. Bring me a mate, Lord." That's not trust; that's foolishness.

There is a time for prayer and also a time for action. You must act on the instructions you receive from God during your times of prayer. You must play your part. You must be wise and allow God to place you in positions where you will meet other people. Everything you do must be done in trust and faith, knowing that God will orchestrate your future, but you must also do your part by obeying His wisdom and His voice.

Back to Psalm 37:3:

> Trust in the LORD, and do good; Dwell in the land and cultivate faithfulness. (NAS)

There is more to this verse than trusting God. It also tells us to do good, dwell in the land, and cultivate faithfulness. Through my years of ministering in America and overseas, I have often heard negative reports about singles in the Church. "Well, you can't count on the singles," I'm told. "You never know if they'll show up or not. And, if they do, they're usually late." That is not a reputation of *doing good*. Of course, not every single behaves this way, but it's evident the singles' culture has given people reason for believing this is to be true.

We must cultivate faithfulness in every area of our lives—first to God and to our church, then to our jobs and relationships with others. If you commit to doing something for your church, follow through with that commitment and keep your word. This is basic character development. Developing faithfulness in all areas of your life will make you a better person. You will become a bigger blessing to those around you and you will present yourself as a person who can be trusted—a character trait one looks for in a mate. I encourage you to use this time of being single to cultivate faithfulness.

Notice also that the verse says, "Dwell in the land." I believe this refers to living in God's will. Just as the Garden of Eden was symbolic of God's perfect will for Adam and Eve, He also wants us to remain in His perfect will for us. He does not want us to wander around looking for a mate in all the wrong places. So when you find the church God has called you to, be faithful and dwell in that land. I take issue with those who feel church hopping is a good way to meet more single people. What if everyone subscribed to that philosophy? How would you know if you hopped in when five other people had just hopped out? Or did you hop out when God was having someone special move into town and hop in?

I'm not saying it's wrong to visit other churches for special meetings. The church down the road may be hosting a seminar or a special retreat for singles. By all means, sign up and go. It is good to take advantage of all such opportunities to meet new people. But it is also wise to be faithful to your local church so the pastor can count on you as an active member. The bottom line in this is to trust and obey God. Trust that when He calls you to a certain church, your obedience and faithfulness to that call will put you in the right place at the right time. Stay planted; be faithful. Earn the reputation of being dependable. It would be great for me to hear in my travels, "If you need something done, ask an unmarried person. They always get the job done. They're on time and never back out of their commitments."

Do your part by doing good, dwelling in the land, cultivating faithfulness, going to special meetings, attending singles' retreats, and whatever else God impresses you to do. Then trust that He will do His part and lead you into His perfect will. I call this *supernatural* living—God's *super* plus your *natural*. This divine partnership will ensure that you become all God has called you to be and you will accomplish all He has called you to do.

All right, you're trusting God, doing good, dwelling in the land, and cultivating faithfulness. But the big question still remains: Are we there yet? How long will it be before I find my true love?

Good question…

Chapter Six

"When, God, When?"

"But as for me, I trust in You, O LORD; I say, 'You are my God.'
My times are in Your hand."
PSALM 31:14-15

Jane's unhappiness and oppression deepened as she approached her twenty-eighth birthday. One question prevailed: "When am I going to find that special someone? I thought for sure I would be married by now." Even though Jane was still single, she had a good life. She served in the ministry as a pastor's assistant. She had no major problems, but still this strange heaviness assailed her. Was she going through an early mid-life crisis?

Jane went to God in prayer and asked Him why she was feeling the oppression that was seemingly linked to her upcoming birthday. The Lord took her back to a memory in junior high school. At that time, there had been a twenty-eight-year-old single woman in her church. Jane remembered that she and her friends had often asked, "What's wrong with that lady? She looks normal. Why can't she get a boyfriend and get married?

She must be strange or something, to be that old and not married." Jane and her friends did not know what the situation was with the woman, but they all concluded that something must be seriously wrong with her.

As Jane reminisced, a thought hit her like a slap in the face. *I'm that lady! I'm going to turn twenty-eight and I'm still single. What's wrong with me? Am I ever going to get married?* There was no longer a question as to why Jane felt oppressed. Years ago, she had placed a mental block in her mind that said if a woman was not married by the time she hit twenty-eight, she was weird.

Jane went back to God in prayer. "God, I'm confused," she cried. "Hello, Father, see me down here? I'm still single. What's going on? Have I missed You somewhere down the road? Am I ever going to get married?" Jane's heart cried out, "When, God, when? When am I ever going to get married?" The more she thought about this, the more depressed she became. She could not help but think about all her friends who were married—many younger than she was and some even had children already. Jane was quickly heading down the path of discouragement.

When can be a dangerous question. Meditating on *when* causes us to focus on our unmet desires instead of releasing them to God and trusting Him to orchestrate the future. The road to depression is paved with that question —When. If one is not careful, "When, God, when?" can steal peace and literally suck joy right from the heart.

Jane had to turn her heart and mind to God through Thank-You Prayers. As hard as it was to let go of her oppression, she called out for God's grace. In the midst of the grace, Thank-You Prayers fell from her lips and peace entered her soul.

> Thank You, Jesus, that my life is in Your hands and You are leading me into Your perfect plan. Lord, I thank You I'm still alive and turning twenty-eight.

Like Jane, we must release our future and the desires it still holds. This means we must stop asking God *when* and start telling Him that we trust Him. I had a similar experience when I approached my late twenties. When I realized I was growing old alone, the thought overwhelmed me. I admit twenty-eight is not old at all, but I was feeling old at the time—old and very single. Things were not going as I had planned. I wanted time to stand still until I found the love of my life and got married. Then the clock could start ticking again. I had planned on being married and having a couple of children by the time I was twenty-eight. That desire and goal was not even in sight.

What helps you get through tough times like this? With God's grace, continue to release your desires to God through Thank-You Prayers. When you do, you will be able to trust Him with your future. Learn to write down your plans in pencil, but then give God the eraser.

Proverbs 16:9 says, "A man's heart plans his way, But the LORD directs his steps."

Decide to let God direct your steps instead of working your own plan. God wants you to release the whole idea of marriage to Him—to give Him your present and trust Him with your future. Psalm 31:14-15a says, "But as for me, I trust in You, O LORD; I say, 'You *are* my God.' My times *are* in Your hand."

> Father, I acknowledge You in all my ways, including still being single. I don't understand why I am still single, but I trust in You with all my heart and I choose not to lean on my own understanding. I give You my life, just the way it is. Thank You for directing my paths. I release the whole idea of marriage to You. My future is in Your hands.

Continue to thank God for all He has done in your life and all He is doing now. Whenever thoughts of "When, God, when" whisper in your ear, turn those whispers into Thank-You Prayers. God will fill you with His grace and turning twenty-eight, thirty, or forty won't seem that bad after all. When you give your life to the Lord, He holds you firmly. So let go and trust God—you're in good hands.

DISCUSSION QUESTIONS

1. Do you have difficulty trusting God with your future? Name some specific areas in which you know you need to trust in God.

2. Are you doing your part by dwelling in God's will and cultivating faithfulness? In what areas of your life do you need to start obeying God?

3. Write a personal Thank-You Prayer you can pray the next time you are tempted to dwell on, "When, God, when?"

Section IV
Got Anger?

Chapter Seven

The Phone Call

"Cease from anger, and forsake wrath"
Psalm 37:8a (NAS)

One day the Lord told me that Psalm 37 was perfect for a single person on his or her journey to marriage. However, when I read verse 8, "Cease from anger, and forsake wrath," I was perplexed as to what anger had to do with anything. I was doubly perplexed when I saw in *Strong's Concordance* that the Hebrew word for *cease* means "*to slacken*" and the word for *anger* means "*to breathe hard through the nose; i.e. to be enraged.*" Then it dawned on me: This might be the feeling a single person gets when he or she receives what I have come to refer to as The Phone Call.

You come home from work to an empty house. You put a frozen dinner in the oven and sit down to watch TV, alone. You see all the happy couples on TV enjoying life together in a state of conjugal bliss. Hoping for 101 messages, you check your voice mail and find *one* message from *one* friend. He just eloped with his girlfriend and is in Hawaii. None of your other friends are around, because they have all gone on a singles' retreat. The telephone rings and hope springs eternal—it's your mom in Idaho asking when you are ever coming home again for a visit.

As you look around your empty home, your heart sinks, and your desire for companionship rises. Ring, ring, ring - it's The Phone Call. Your friend, Susie, is on the other end.

"Hello, Susie, how are you?"

"I'm absolutely wonderful. Never been so excited in my life!"

"And why is that?" you ask.

"I'M GETTING MARRIED!"

From the thumping sound, you know she's jumping up and down doing the victory dance. You have mixed emotions, but muster up a selfless response of joy. "You mean it? You're really engaged? That's so nice to hear. Congratulations."

But, your thoughts are: *I can't believe this. This is a night from hell. I thought for sure I would get married before Susie. She's five years younger than I am! Lord, when is it going to be my turn?*

This type of phone call seems to become more feared as you advance in age. It was for me. I remember when a friend called me to announce his engagement and asked me to be in his wedding. I offered my congratulations and told him how happy I was for him. However, to be honest, something totally different was going on inside. *No, I do not want to be in your wedding,* my heart cried, *I want you in MY wedding!* Let's be real. For most singles, being in someone else's wedding is not the most fun thing to do. I remember thinking:

"Sure, I'd love to be in your wedding. I can't wait to buy a $300 ticket to fly to your city. Rent a car for the weekend for $150 and spend another $200 for a hotel. Spend $125 on a tuxedo that won't fit and will make me itch all day. Fork out another $100 bucks on a gift for you and your bride, just so I can fly home to my empty apartment. Yeah, love to. There's nothing

I'd rather spend the $875 on anyway. Not that I *need* a surround sound system."

Of course it is not really about the money, but it is common to experience mixed emotions when hearing someone else's wedding announcement. "God, I'm happy for Susie, but when do I get to make the call announcing MY engagement? I feel like the only single person on the face of the earth."

What do you do when you receive phone calls like this? How do you get through the mixed emotions? Remember Philippians 4:6, "In every situation, with thanksgiving, let your requests be made known to God." Getting a phone call announcing someone else's wedding is surely a situation. How about turning it over to God in prayer?

> Thank You, Jesus, my future is in Your hands.
> Thank You my turn is coming in Your timing.

Even in the midst of unexpected phone calls announcing a friend's engagement, you can have peace. You can even get to the point of being excited for your friends who are getting married.

God does not want you to live with anger every time you are reminded that you are still single. We may think we are angry at the situation, but in fact, the anger can be traced back to anger toward God Himself. If we were painfully honest, we would admit that when we get angry, we are really saying, "God, why haven't You met this desire yet? What are You waiting for?" This is not a healthy position to be in. So take the psalmist David's advice, slacken your breathing and let go of anger.

> Father, thank You that my times are in Your hands. Thank You for leading me to my true love and giving me a beautiful marriage. Your Word says as I wait patiently on You that You will strengthen my heart. Thank You for filling me with Your strength. Thank You that one day

I can make this same call to all my friends; but in the meantime, I trust You and choose to enjoy the journey.

Experiencing The Phone Call is one thing. Then there are the Romeos and Juliets who seem to flaunt their happy-ever-after couple status right in front of you. They can really get your nostrils flaring. The devil does not play fair either. It seems he lies low for a while, and at the opportune time, he pounces! For me, an attack would usually hit around Valentine's Day.

CHAPTER EIGHT

The Valentine Blues

"That should be illegal!"

After my college girlfriend and I broke up, I decided I was going to stop playing the dating game and wait to date my mate. For nine years before I met my wife, Pippa, there were times I experienced what I have come to call the Valentine Blues. Have you ever gone to a movie alone? If you have, you know what I'm talking about. Inevitably, Mr. and Mrs. Happy-Ever-After sit right in front of you. They don't care what movie is playing. They're just there to ruin it for you with their "we're so in love" looks. Their holding hands and kissy pecks on the neck are enough to irritate any single person. You start breathing a little hard through the nose. You feel like leaning forward and whispering to them in a loud voice, "Do you mind? I'm still single, and your blissful attitude is making me sick!"

Sometimes the sight of married or dating couples can trigger a chain reaction on the inside. February seems to be one of the toughest months. Valentine's Day is not something most singles mark on their calendar and look forward to with warm fuzzies. Usually during this season, people think, "Here we go *again*. When am I ever going to have that special someone I can buy roses for? I thought for sure I'd be married or at least dating my future mate by now." You try your best to look at the bright side. "Well, at least I'm saving some money, *again*." Although, the honest truth be known, you're angry. You would have rather been married to your true love so you could lavish him or her with gifts and affection on Valentine's Day.

So what do you do when valentine fever begins to spread through the air every February? Get depressed? Walk around complaining and getting angry with God? Worse, do you find a partner just so you can celebrate the big day and not have to put up with all your friends and family saying "Poor Susie, still no valentine?"

Or, on the other hand, do you look to Jesus?

I remember one day sitting in my car, all alone, waiting for the light to turn green. I was about twenty-eight years old at the time, still single as a dollar bill. In the truck in front of me was a young couple. He was driving, and the woman, well, she was practically sitting on the guy's lap. They were laughing and looking at each other all starry-eyed, with these ridiculous in-love smirks on their faces. It was enough to make me gag.

"You should get over in your own seat, woman," I thought. "What do you think this is, a drive-in theater?" I was doing all right for a while, but then I swear I could read their lips: "I love you. I'm so happy we have each other. I'm so glad I'm not single and pathetically lonely like that guy behind us." Well, I'm not sure if that was it exactly, but that's what I imagined. I began to breathe a little harder. Then it got worse. The two lovebirds started kissing each other right in front of me.

"Get in your seat, and keep your hands and lips to yourself," I grumbled. "That should be illegal!" I was experiencing the blues big time and breathing heavily through my nose by now.

The whole feeling of being the only single person on the face of the earth overwhelmed me.

"Why didn't you just go out and get a girlfriend so you could kiss someone?" you may ask. I probably could have done that, and many people do. But, I had set a standard for myself that the next person I dated was going to be my wife. I wasn't interested in giving my heart away to a person I was not going to marry nor in starting a relationship for the selfish reason of having a partner to kiss.

Just when I thought the situation at the traffic light could not get any worse, it did. The light turned green. Did the two romantics see it? Noooo! They were too busy locking lips and enjoying life! I got really angry. My heart began to beat hard and with nostrils flaring, I ignited, "That's it! That's going too far!" (Now, I wish I could tell you I just sat there waiting patiently for this sweet little couple to realize the light was green, but I cannot.)

What did I do? What do you think I did? Yep, HONK-HONK-HONK! I honked my horn politely, but firmly enough to let them know the light was green and to get moving! If 212° is boiling, I was about 205° at this point. Of course they ceased kissing, looked around startled, and drove off.

I felt fairly good about myself. "Do that in front of me. I'll show you..."

Then I heard the Holy Spirit softly ask, "What was that?" Attempting to justify my actions I responded, "Ahh, the light *was* green, God. She didn't even have her seatbelt on, God. I was just trying to help."

It sounded good to me. I was just a concerned citizen trying to protect and serve my fellow man. Then the silence of God filled the car. (Have you ever heard the silence of God? That's louder than anything!) I thought my excuses had sufficed, but I was left there challenged to face what had just happened. I had a choice. I could let this anger stew in me and bother me all day and let the blues set in, or I could slacken my breathing and look to Jesus.

By God's grace, I turned my frustration into peace with Thank-You Prayers. I took a deep breath and began to thank the Lord for sending me the right person at the right time. I thanked Him for leading and guiding me. I thanked Him for saving me from the pain of wrong relationships over the years. I began to thank Him for having my future in His hands. My heart rate slowed and so did my breathing. I was ceasing from anger. I prayed:

> Thank You, Jesus, that one day I can sit at a red light and give my wife a big long kiss and not even care if the light turns green. Furthermore, I hope the same couple that was just in front of me is behind me at the time! (Hey, nobody's perfect.)

Get yourself laughing! Change your attitude, and change the whole situation to one of hope and trust in God. You do not have to allow what you see to anger you and rob you of your joy. Replacing anxious thoughts and angry emotions with Thank-You Prayers will help you enjoy even the most difficult seasons of your life. The next time you find yourself starting to breathe hard because you see two lovebirds perched on the fence of bliss, turn the anger into a Thank-You Prayer.

When I changed my conversation from complaining to thanksgiving, the atmosphere in my car changed. Confusion, stress, and anger were all exchanged with God's peace. My heart was filled with joy for the present, along with great expectation for the future.

The fact is, you do not have to let anger get the best of you; you do not have to experience the valentine blues. When thoughts of loneliness, frustration, and anger come, turn them all into thanksgiving.

I know praying a Thank-You Prayer does not change your circumstances or your marital status. However, thanksgiving will make way for your heart to receive God's peace and manifested presence. Remember, getting angry or stressed out does not change your circumstances, either. If neither one changes my situation, I am going to choose thanksgiving, so I can have peace instead of living a life full of frustration. The choice is yours.

God has you in His hands and He is orchestrating a special plan for your life. Jeremiah 29:11 tells us, " 'For I know the plans I have for you,' declares the LORD, plans to prosper you and not to harm you, plans to give you hope and a future" (NIV).

I challenge you to turn your anger and blues into thanksgiving, not only during the Valentine's Day season, but also throughout your daily life. If you do, you will be able to join the Apostle Paul in saying, "I have learned how to be content (satisfied to the point where I am not disturbed or disquieted) in whatever state I am" (Philippians 4:11 AMP).

It is important to remember that a fulfilled life does not begin when you receive a desire, achieve a dream, or get married. A fulfilled life begins when you give your life to Jesus and seek to know Him. He, and He alone, will satisfy.

> Thank You, Jesus, that my future is in Your hands. You are orchestrating the timing of everything and in that I rest. I will not torture myself trying to figure it all out. Instead, I roll my future and my desires upon You. Please take my anger and replace it with Your peace. I know You love me and want what is best for me.
>
> Forgive me for getting angry with You and not trusting You completely. According to Your Word, my steps are ordered of You and You will lead me into Your perfect will. Thank You for Your grace that enables me to release my desire to be married and wait patiently on Your timing. I will not allow my unknown future to rob my

present joy. In You I am complete and in You I am fulfilled. Jesus, I love You. Amen.

And then, just when you think you have a handle on the anger issue, in come the matchmakers of this world.

Chapter Nine

The Matchmakers

"No, we are not getting married; we're just sitting together!"

Sometimes people don't make the journey any easier on singles. I used to hate it when I was invited to what I thought was a simple dinner, only to discover it was a set-up in the works. Bill and his lovely wife wink at each other with a twinkle in their eyes. They have a smirk on their faces that says they know something you don't. They seem overly, but quietly, excited as they pull out the chair for you that is strategically situated next to someone of the opposite sex whom you have never met.

"Oh, hi, Mike! Glad you could make it to dinner tonight. You know my wife Lynn, and this is Debra, Lynn's friend from work. She's up for an executive promotion, has a great personality, her own home, and just happened to be in the neighborhood."

You muster up a smile, but on the inside you're saying, "Liar, liar pants on fire!"

Friends aren't the only culprits. Even church folks you barely know play the role of matchmaker. Have you noticed that it is hard to sit with another single of the opposite sex in church without people marrying you two?

One Sunday you decide to sit with a friend of the opposite gender. On your way out of church Mrs. Jones stops you. "You two make such a sweet couple," she says with a grin. "I'm so happy for you."

"Happy about what?" you ask.

"Oh, I saw you sitting together at church this morning," she responds. "I think it's great that you have finally found someone special."

You slowly respond, "Ah, ma'am, we're just friends. We just decided to sit together."

It almost looks like tears are welling up in her eyes as she says, "That's so sweet." Then she hugs you tightly. As you walk through the foyer you notice others looking at you with silly grins and whispering to each other as you pass.

It is even worse when the ushers are in cahoots. They rotate sitting you by another single person each week hoping to solve your "problem." It's a conspiracy. In fact, last week when you sat by one of your friends of the opposite sex, you probably noticed the entire congregation giving you the thumbs up.

I don't know about you, but all that used to irk me big time. It was the smirk that really got to me. The smirk that said so much more than words: "This may be the one for you, Jeff." Or, "I'm so happy you found someone. I know you must be miserable as a single person, but now you can start living a life filled with joy and happiness." All this, because I sat with the same woman two Sundays in a row!

I am frequently asked, "What can I do about people trying to set me up? What can I do when people start talking and pairing me off with someone just because I sit with them in church?"

My answer: Nothing.

You cannot stop people from talking or strategizing your "love connection." I suppose you could try. You could write a letter to everyone you know telling them you will never go out to dinner with them again unless they sign a written contract stating that you will be the only guest with no surprises. You could go to every person in your church and explain that just because you sit with someone two Sundays in a row does not mean you are getting married. Then you could do it all over again when you happen to sit with someone else. You could have the pastor announce your platonic relationship from the pulpit or even put a blurb in the bulletin next to your pictures.

Or, you could slacken your breathing and turn the concern into peace through Thank-You Prayers. Thank-You Prayers will help you release what others do and say about you, thus rendering their words and actions ineffective in your life. You cannot control what others say and do, but you *can* control how it affects you.

If you want to, it is probably not a bad idea to share your heart with people close to you. Be open and honest with them. Let them know you're uncomfortable when they try to set you up with someone or make comments when you sit with a single person of the opposite sex. Those closest to you should understand and honor your wishes. However, do not be totally closed to sincere, heartfelt assistance from others. God can always use other people to help orchestrate His plan for your life.

This aspect of a single's life is just another good opportunity to turn situations into prayer and trust God. In spite of times of awkward matchmaking assistance from others, God will lead you as you trust Him and grow more intimate with Him. The next time somebody's actions or comments make you feel awkward and angry, close the door on anger and open the door to God's peace through prayer. Prayer will help you keep your eyes on the Lord. When your eyes are on Him, you will be able to breathe easy and enjoy any journey in life.

Thank You, Jesus, that Your eye is upon me at all times. You see all I go through and the challenges I face. I choose to commit my life to You afresh today, leaving no room for anger or hurt. I release others and what they say about me. Thank You that their words do not harm me or affect me in any way. I choose to set my thoughts on You and I thank You for Your peace.

DISCUSSION QUESTIONS

1. Have you ever received The Phone Call? How did you honestly feel? Discuss and write down a Thank-You Prayer that will help you next time The Phone Call rings at your home.

2. Is valentine's season tough for you? Do you have any "red light" stories of your own? Discuss how you handled it and how you felt. Did you get angry? Sad? Frustrated?

3. Discuss and write down a Thank-You Prayer that would help you in the future when anger or frustration knocks on the door of your heart.

4. Have you ever been the victim of well-intended matchmakers? How did it make you feel?

Section V
Resting in the Lord

CHAPTER TEN

The Dating Game

*"Commit your way to the LORD.
Rest in the LORD and wait patiently for Him."*
PSALM 37:5A,7A (NAS)

Loneliness, the pitfalls of dating, and the big "How do you know if he or she is the right one?" all play a major role in hindering the rest God wants all singles to enjoy. Notice the progression in Psalm 37 verses 5 and 7. First you commit your way to the Lord, then comes rest. The word *commit* means "to roll." It is the same word that is used in Proverbs 16:3,

> Roll your works upon the Lord [commit them wholly to Him; He will cause your thoughts to become agreeable to His will, and] so shall your plans be established *and* succeed. (AMP)

When we commit an area of our lives to the Lord, it is no longer in our hands to control; it's in His hands. And when something is in God's hands, He is able to orchestrate His plan. The way God does this is by giving us wisdom and causing our thoughts to become agreeable to His will. When we listen to wisdom and think according to God's will, the next part of the verse comes into play: "So shall your plans be established and succeed."

When we commit our ways to the Lord and follow His wisdom, our success rate increases tremendously. One great way to commit something to the Lord and then leave it in His hands is through praying Thank-You Prayers. In the next few chapters we will look at three areas every single needs to commit to the Lord in order to receive His rest: Dating; How you "just know" when the right one comes along; and Loneliness.

THE DATING GAME

One of the toughest challenges a single person who desires a mate faces is: "Who am I going to marry?" Therefore, it is one of the most difficult to commit to the Lord. "Is it the guy at work who has shown an interest in me? What about my good friend, George. Could he be the one? What about the new accountant at church? She's really good-looking."

I once had a single friend who couldn't sit through a meal at a restaurant without checking out every waitress wondering if she was the one for him. "She has blond hair; I like blond hair. She is over five feet tall, that's good. No ring on the finger. She even smiled at me." There were a number of times that my friend even got the waitress' phone number before leaving. He couldn't stop wondering about who he was going to marry.

"Who" is the big unknown in every person's heart until the wedding ring is slipped on the finger. Over the years, Western civilization has come up with a method of finding a mate that is basically a process of elimination. Some call it the dating game.

It goes like this. Date this one for a while to see if he will do. If not, date the next one and the next one, until you find one you think you could live with for a lifetime. It's a fault-ridden method that usually fails and causes undesirable consequences. However costly this game is, most people, saved and unsaved alike, engage in it all the time. Many lives are riddled with pain and confusion due to this unwise approach to relationships.

Our lives are made up of all kinds of relationships. Therefore, the decisions you make in this area are extremely important. The greatest pain and the greatest joy you will experience in life will come as a result of a relationship. Therefore, it would serve you well to commit this whole area to the Lord. If you do, you will make room for His wisdom to help you make wise choices that will ensure a joy-filled future.

Lori wept as she hung up the phone. After a year of dating, Bobby told her he wanted to be "just friends." "Why does this always happen to me?" Lori cried. "I told myself I would never let another guy hurt me like this. That's it; I'm never dating again!"

Even though many have learned how painful the dating game can be, the lack of knowledge and the desire for lifelong companionship drives them to keep playing. If you have gone through several dating relationships, you have probably said these words: "There's got to be a better way."

The big problem with the dating game is that we are playing with something much more serious than we realize. Dating involves two people's hearts, and a heart is no toy. When two people start dating seriously—become boyfriend and girlfriend—something happens. Their hearts begin to intimately tie themselves together with cords of love, hoping to never come apart. Rightfully so. God never intended one's heart to be tied to someone, only to be ripped apart six months or a year later.

Developing a relationship is like building a house. The Bible says in Luke 14:28, "What kind of man starts building a building when he knows he does not have enough materials to finish it?" (Paraphrased) I call this the principle of process. Don't start a process unless you know you can finish it in the way it is intended to be finished.

That's why I believe wisdom would say, "Wait to date your mate." Don't start building a house with someone until you know that he or she will be the one who will finish it with you. In other words, don't tie your heart to another in a boyfriend/girlfriend relationship until you find the one you believe God has called you to marry.

We have all heard the phrase, "tying the knot." Well, the tying of the knot did not start on the wedding day—it was being tied for months. If a dating relationship does not end in marriage, there are still knots tied. Multitudes of people live with knots in their hearts *and* stomachs due to broken relationships.

I have talked to people who are not even saved who have come to this wise conclusion. "I'm tired of this dating stuff. The next person I give my heart to will be my future mate." It does not make sense to start building a house only to tear it down halfway through the process.

The sad thing is that most people arrive at this conclusion only after deep pain, rather than by listening to wisdom in the first place. Many think they are somehow unique and will be able to avoid the inevitable consequences of unwise relationships. "I won't get hurt. I can handle it," they assure themselves. The problem is that we are not made to handle it! God did not give anyone a special quality exempting them from pain when ending an intimate relationship. The best way is to commit the idea of dating to the Lord and learn from wisdom instead of painful experience.

Think of the dating relationship as a process, similar to eating a meal. Like all processes, by definition, there is a beginning and an end. If you were to come to my house around 5:30 in the evening, you probably would find my wife, Pippa, cooking a meal. The first thing to hit you would be the aroma of garlic bread and sautéed onions. Noodles boiling and sauces simmering would tell you that she was cooking spaghetti for dinner.

"Hey Pippa, looks like you're cooking a meal."

Wiping perspiration from her forehead, Pippa replies, "Yep, I'm cooking a fine meal."

"So, you and Jeff are going to eat spaghetti tonight, right?"

Checking the garlic bread for the last time, Pippa turns and says, "Nope, I'm just having fun. I thought I would start cooking it, and then throw it all away."

Out of concern, you might give the cook a little friendly advice. "Pippa, it would probably be best to wait to start cooking a meal until you and Jeff are ready to eat it."

Though tongue-in-cheek, the wisdom of the principle of process is obvious in preparing for a meal, but what about a relationship? Do you know how many people are cooking a relationship without any idea whether they will actually be partaking of it in the future? The boyfriend/girlfriend dating relationship is a process intended to end in marriage. As found in Luke 14, the principle of process teaches one to not enter the process of dating until he or she is ready and willing to accept the end result. Wisdom would say wait to date your mate and that means waiting to date the person you will marry.

When wisdom and patience are not used, processes are begun and not completed. Not finishing a process as it is intended will bring undesirable results—waste of time, resources, energy, and even money, among other things. Dating breakups add emotional damage, guilt, insecurity, and self-doubt.

The next time your hormones and emotions compel you to start dating, remember what wisdom would say: "This is not a game. Is he or she the one I will finish the process with and marry?" If your answer is *No* or *I don't know*, remain friends and stay out of the dating process until you do know. Commit thoughts of needing a dating partner to the Lord through Thank-You Prayers.

> Father, thank You that You have a better way for me to find my future mate than the dating game. Thank You that I do not have to tie my

heart to multiple partners in order to find "Mr. or Miss Right." Thank You that when I commit my ways in relationships to You, You cause my thoughts to become agreeable to Your will. Thank You for helping me have successful relationships through wise decisions.

The common phrase used to end dating relationships is actually the best place to keep things from the beginning—"just friends." If you stop playing the game and listen to simple wisdom, you will enjoy life more and avoid painful pitfalls. Proverbs 13:14 says: "The teaching of the wise is a fountain of life, that one may avoid the snares of death" (AMP).

When the dating game is played, people set themselves up for a lot of hurt and anxiety. It's better to keep things at the friendship level until you have heard God tell you to pursue the dating process with the partner He has chosen for you.

"But Jeff, what do I do in the meantime?" you ask. Begin by committing your life to the Lord. Then, with God's grace, practice the principles you have learned in this book. Whenever you get worried about not knowing whom you are going to marry, roll your worries onto God with Thank-You Prayers. Replace anxiety with the peace of God and continue to pursue friendships while trusting God to bring you your special someone.

Every time you get discouraged because you see two people kissing, holding hands, or gazing into each other's eyes, say, "Thank You, Jesus. I know You are directing my paths." Look to Jesus to be your partner and to fulfill your emotional needs. Remember, no one can complete you more than God can.

Father, thank You that when I commit the whole idea of dating to You, I can enter rest, knowing You will take care of me. Thank You for leading and guiding me in Your will and helping me to avoid the temptations of unwise dating.

Chapter Eleven

How Do You Know If You Have Found the Right One?

"What do you mean you just know?"

Nearly everywhere I go in my ministry travels, I am asked the age-old question: "How do I know if he or she is the right one?" I hear this in Mexico, Finland, England, and all over America. Even in Zimbabwe, it pops up. This question can be a source of great stress for any single person.

When I was single and believing God for a mate, I asked the same question of my married friends. I hated the answer most couples gave me. Usually the couple would look at each other with this "we're so in love" smirk, then turn back to me, and in unison say, "You just know." I would get totally frustrated. "You just know! You just know. What do you mean you just know?"

However, after meeting my wife and going through the process, I must confess I see what they meant. After getting to know Pippa, I too gained an internal knowing that she was the one for me. Now, I give the same "you just know" answer, because ultimately it is the best one. (I try to avoid the whole "we're so in love" smirk, though.) Trust me, when you get married, you'll probably be giving the same answer.

The best way I can explain the concept of "you just know," is by asking you a couple of questions. Are you saved? How do you know you are saved? Most people say, "Because the Bible says if you confess with your mouth…." That's nice, but how do you know the Bible is true and salvation is real? Eventually most people shrug their shoulders and say, "I just know!" The same way you "just know" that you are saved is the same way you will "just know" what God's will is for your life in other areas, including whom you are to marry.

However, remembering how "you just know" never satisfied me, I asked God to give me some pointers on more practical ways singles could discern Mr. or Miss Right. The following are a couple of ways to help you discern if a person is the right one to marry.

A Growing Inner Peace

You need to be sure you are being led by a peace that grows, not a feeling that comes and goes. The key here is a *growing* inner peace. Whenever God speaks to you, He will reveal a path of increasing peace and what He says will stick with you over the course of time. In speaking of wisdom, Proverbs 3:17b says, "and all her paths are peace."

I remember when a missionary from South America visited our church. After hearing him preach, I knew for sure I was being called to the mission field. About three weeks later, however, I no longer sensed the calling. As long as the missionary was there preaching, I was packing my bags; but when he left, so did my peace. If God had called me to be a missionary, it would have stuck with me even in the absence of the preacher. Also, the feeling of peace about my going to the mission field would have grown, not dwindled.

God operates the same way when letting us know who He wants us to marry or even start dating. He does not lead us through the human feelings we get when we are with the person; God leads with a peace that grows and a knowing that stays. Colossians 3:15a says,

> Let the peace (soul harmony which comes) from Christ rule (act as umpire continually) in your hearts [deciding and settling with finality all questions that arise in your minds, in that peaceful state]. (AMP)

Notice this verse does not say let your feelings rule in your heart.

"But brother Jeff, it feels so right when I am with him," you tell me. "I just never want to let him go." Of course it *feels* good. The problem with relying on a feeling is that another guy down the road can make you *feel* good, too. Is that the leading of God, or your God-given hormones talking? So, how can you tell the difference between an inner peace and a good feeling? One way is to use the method outlined in the next point—a fast.

THE RELATIONSHIP MUST SURVIVE A FAST.

We all know what a fast is when it comes to food. A food fast is a period of time during which you consecrate yourself and refrain from eating. You take the time you normally spend eating to seek God and draw closer to Him. And, by denying your flesh, you sharpen your spiritual sensitivity to God's voice.

I believe every couple headed for marriage needs to survive a relationship fast, especially if they are engaged. I encourage couples to separate themselves for a period of time and really seek God for His will on the relationship. I recommend a fast of at least seven days. During a relationship fast, you do not see each other. You do not talk to each other. You do not e-mail each other or have any contact whatsoever. You also do not read old love letters your partner has written. You even put away his or her pictures. When you fast the relationship, you create a season of total separation from your partner. If you think there is absolutely no way that you could spend seven days without your partner, I suggest you go seek Christian counsel on the subject of codependency.

What happens during this fast can literally save your life. At the very least, you will grow more intimate with the Lord. You may or may not experience a strengthening of your inner peace. Furthermore, you may discover that the strong feelings you have when you are with that person have been suffocating God's voice in your life. The fast takes you out of a position where feelings can cloud your vision of good judgment and into a position to more accurately hear the voice of God. During the fast, ask God to give you Scriptures that confirm His will for you in the relationship. Do not be closed to what He would say. Sincerely seek His will above everything—even your own feelings. Let God know you want to hear Him, no matter what He might say.

When your heart and mind are on the Lord instead of your dating partner, you are in a better position to hear God's voice.

> Thank You, Jesus, that I hear Your voice and no other voice will I follow. Thank You for helping me separate my emotions from this relationship and consecrate myself unto You. I ask You to reveal to me Your will for this relationship. My utmost desire is to please and honor You in all I do.

If you diligently seek God during your fast, He will speak to you concerning His will. You must then make a quality decision to obey whatever He tells you to do. You want to be led by God's voice, not human feelings. Why? Because faith is the only thing that will keep a marriage together for a lifetime. The Bible says faith comes by hearing and hearing by the Word of God. When things get tough in marriage (and they will), it won't be your feelings that keep you together. It will be the faith that came from hearing God say, "This person is the one I want you to marry."

Some people readily see the wisdom of a relationship fast while others may need time to pray about it and absorb the idea. You do not want to go to your partner and demandingly say, "Hey, I am going to fast this relationship and I will see you in a couple weeks." That won't go over very well.

Prayerfully prepare yourself before presenting this idea to your partner. Then, with God's grace, humbly present the idea in a loving way. Include in your presentation your love for the other person and your desire to make sure you are hearing God correctly about the relationship. Your partner must hear your tender heart and realize you are presenting this concept out of love for him or her and for the desire to be in God's will.

It would be wise to consider showing your partner this section of the book about the relationship fast. (In fact, if you are dating, you should be reading this book together!) Your goal is to come into agreement that it is wise to seek God's will in the relationship.

After presenting the idea of fasting the relationship, ask your partner to prayerfully consider the idea. It is possible that your partner may feel rejected or hurt by the mere suggestion of separating for a period of time. If you see this happen, reassure him or her of your love and remind him or her that it is love that is prompting the idea. Give your partner time to absorb the idea and pray. If your partner blows up in anger or continues to be resistant, you need to ask yourself the question: Do you really want to pursue a relationship with a person who doesn't honor your request for the fast and who lacks the desire to do what it takes to accurately hear God?

After at least seven days of your fast, meet together in a public place where you can discuss what each person has experienced. If the relationship has been confirmed in your heart with an increased peace, share that with your partner. Then you must listen to and respect what your partner has to say. If one person believes it is time to put a hold on the relationship, the other must back off even if he or she does not agree.

If one partner discounts the other's fast experience or decrees his or her own experience the only valid one, then the relationship has problems that will be harder to wrestle with if a union is made. If your partner's opinion is completely different than yours, logic dictates there is something not quite right.

If you love someone, you want him or her in the center of God's will. The point of the fast is to put you and your partner in a position to accurately hear God about the relationship. Not only that, but your willingness to fast the relationship demonstrates that God, not your partner, is still the center of your life.

There are many other factors we could look at to help you discern God's will for your life in a relationship. We could talk about the growing unselfish love and the ability to work through problems. We could also talk about the importance of gaining the agreement of those we see as counselors in our lives.

Still the age-old question haunts singles—*How do you know?* You come to know through your walk with Jesus and listening to His wisdom.

The best advice I can give is to direct you to the presence of God. Hunger after God and develop an intimate relationship with Him. The closer you are to the Lord, the more accurately you discern His voice—not only for the question of whom to marry, but in every area of life. A person walking in intimacy with the Lord will "just know." I am not saying that you will know the first time you meet the person, but over time, God's peace will lead you. We must be led by His peace, not by feelings. Many times a separation is needed to accurately discover what God is saying to your heart about the relationship.

Whom you are going to marry is the most important decision you will ever make second to your decision to give your life to Jesus. Knowing who that right person is begins with committing your life to God and allowing Him to cause your thoughts to become agreeable to His will. Do not wait until you meet someone you like to commit this area to the Lord and to seek God. There are no quick formulas for hearing God; hearing His voice is simply a by-product of well-developed intimacy.

Whenever stress comes from not knowing the answers to the questions, "Who am I going to marry?" and "How will I know if he or she is the right one for me," commit the questions to God and enter into rest through Thank-You Prayers. Exchange stress for God's peace. Psalm 25:14 says, "The secret of the LORD is with those who fear Him, And He will show them His covenant." When we focus on knowing Christ, we'll hear His secrets, including whom we are to marry.

> Thank You, Lord, that Your sheep hear Your voice. I thank You that when I meet and get to know my future mate, in Your timing, we will both "just know." In the meantime, thank You for helping me become more intimate with You so I can recognize Your voice when You speak to me in every area of my life.

CHAPTER TWELVE

Leave Loneliness Alone

"Marriage is not the ultimate cure for loneliness."

Countless people experience the very real emotion of loneliness. At my live seminars, I ask participants to fill out a questionnaire. One of the questions is, "In your opinion, what is the greatest challenge of being single?" Loneliness is one of the biggest responses. I would safely guess that you have been lonely at times in your single years as well. For me, loneliness seemed to strike in particular situations. As long as I was working hard and traveling in the ministry, loneliness was not much of an issue. But when I returned from a trip to my empty home, my heart longed for companionship.

Feelings of loneliness sometimes crept in when I had to prepare a meal. That was something I did not enjoy doing in the first place. Having to eat the meal alone added to my dismay. The other time loneliness seemed to often attack was when I went to bed. Staring at the ceiling, I would let my heart ponder my marital status a little too long. I remember times when tears dripped from my eyes as loneliness slowly turned into a sense of hopelessness that prevented me from falling asleep. "God, I don't want to be alone any more," I would cry. "I know *You* are with me, but let's face it, it's not the same." The Holy Spirit would try to comfort me with words from Psalm 37:5 and 7: "Commit your way to the Lord and rest in Him." But, to be honest, I didn't want to *rest in Him*. I wanted a mate! However, I also wanted to enjoy where I was—single—on the way to where I wanted to be—married.

The Holy Spirit was right; I needed to commit the idea of my being alone to the Lord and ask Him for His rest. Somehow, by God's grace, Thank-You Prayers would rise in my heart. Sometimes with quivering lips and a frog in my throat, I would muster up something like this:

> Father, thank You for being with me. Thank You for all You have done for me and all You have planned. I commit to You the fact that I am still single and perhaps well beyond the age I wanted to be when I got married. I trust You for Your rest now as I fall asleep in Your arms tonight.

When you look to the Lord in times of despair, your own Thank-You Prayers will emerge.

Webster defines *lonely* as "unhappy at being alone." Something else goes hand in hand with loneliness: boredom. Boredom often opens the door for feelings of loneliness. If boredom and being alone are the primary sources of lonely feelings, let's look at what we can do to solve the problem. Here are some suggestions:

DEVELOP FRIENDSHIPS

One key to developing and maintaining friendships is to *plan* to get together with friends. Too many times we get so busy with work, or simply do not put any effort into planning, that weeks go by and we never get around to doing things with friends. You have to make a date and put it on the calendar. Don't just wait for things to come your way. Look for opportunities to meet others and develop good friendships.

If loneliness is simply the sad feeling of being alone, then create situations where you are not alone. When I was single, there were times I would come home and watch TV for hours, all the while feeling sorry for myself because I was not married. I felt so alone and bored; all the while I had friends who would have loved to play tennis or go to a movie and hang out. All I had to do was call them.

A couple of years ago when I was preparing to write an article for singles, I specifically asked God how I could minister to those who were lonely. I heard the Lord say, "Tell them to leave loneliness alone." I pictured a man sitting on the couch watching TV by himself. He was sad and lonely. Then I pictured him saying, "Thank You, Jesus, I don't have to be lonely. Thank You for helping me leave loneliness alone." Then he got up, left loneliness sitting there, and called some friends to get together. Many times the emotion of loneliness can be overcome by a simple act of our will.

Another thing that helped me overcome loneliness was getting a roommate (of the same sex, of course). I had roommates two different times while I was single. Both were a blessing. I know it is not the same as being married, but it sure took away a lot of boring, empty-home evenings.

ATTEND CHURCH AND SPECIAL EVENTS—
START A SINGLES' MINISTRY!

Attending church and special events will make way for you to develop friendships that, in return, help you overcome loneliness. When I talk about loneliness at my seminars, I know there are probably hundreds of singles who heard about the conference, but chose not to come. Many of them probably sat home feeling lonely. Instead, they could have come to the seminar, had a great time with other people, and even found new friends.

Church is probably the best place for Christians to meet new people and develop relationships. Make an effort to attend church every time the doors open. As you approach the front doors of your church, say, "Thank You, Jesus, for helping me meet new friends. Thank You for giving me confidence and ordering my steps. When I walk through these doors, thank You for being with me."

Get involved in the helps ministry. Ask to join the usher ministry or sign up to help in the children's or youth departments. In addition, invite friends to get together after church or plan an evening together so you can really develop sound friendships. When you hear of special events going on in your area, make plans to attend and invite others.

Don't wait for the pastoral staff to start a singles' ministry and organize events. So many times I've been asked, "What do I do to meet new people? My church does not have a singles' ministry?" My answer: Start one! Talk to your pastor and ask him or her if you can organize and announce a singles' event for next month. Most pastors would love to have you organize such events. The event does not have to be a major thing, either. Simply organizing a get-together at a restaurant after a Sunday night service is a great way to develop friendships and meet new people. You don't need a singles pastor to do that.

For that matter, maybe God is calling you to work alongside your pastoral staff to develop a consistent meeting for singles. You don't need a Bible college degree to start a ministry to singles in your church. After my first year of college, I went home to Rockford, Illinois for the summer. I didn't feel comfortable in the youth group at my church anymore, but there wasn't a ministry for singles. I asked the pastor if I could use a room on Wednesday nights to meet with the singles. He said yes. I had no idea what I was doing or how to head up such a ministry; I just wanted to do something with people my age. We began to meet and the Lord did some great ministry.

One man's life was totally changed at our first meeting. At the end of the meeting, I asked if anyone needed prayer. Two people responded. We stood around them to pray. I felt impressed to ask a particular man to pray for one of the people. He voiced a heartfelt prayer and we all went home. Little did I know that something great had taken place. The man who prayed told me later that his life had been changed at that meeting. "I don't know if you know this or not, Jeff," he began, "but last week at the singles' meeting when you asked me to pray, it was the first time in my life I had ever prayed out loud in a crowd. I have always been too shy or afraid to do it. But when you asked me, I didn't want to say *no*, so I just started talking to God out loud. I felt such a release in my life. Thanks for organizing the meeting and asking me to pray."

Just like that, God changed a life. I was only twenty years old at the time. Simply taking the initiative to organize a meeting opened the door for God to move. When you overcome fear and put yourself in a position to meet people and develop relationships, you will overcome deep feelings of loneliness.

JOIN A CLUB

A fitness center is a great place to have fun and meet other people. One friend of mine joined a tennis team that had matches almost every week. He was happily busy and certainly not bored. Maybe there is a gym or workout center you can join. Ask around. Find out what other people are involved in and see if you can join them.

GET A HOBBY, START A PROJECT, OR JOIN A CLASS

Having a hobby really helps with the boredom issue. (And by the way, watching TV does not qualify as a hobby.) What do you like doing? Is there anything you would like to try? Photography? How about fishing or boating? I've always thought skydiving would be cool.

One day my friend Chris pulled up with what looked like an overgrown surfboard on top of his jeep. "What's that?" I asked.

"Hop in. I'll show you."

He and another friend and I drove to the lake to have what turned out to be one of the most memorable days of our single years. It was a sailboard. You should have seen us trying to stand on that thing! Lord help us if even a slight breeze blew. That was over ten years ago, and to this day, Chris still windsurfs all over the Southeast.

Trying something new, starting a challenging project, or joining a class will help you leave loneliness behind. I can't list every possible hobby in this book, but hopefully I have triggered your imagination. Contact your local college, hobby store, or art store for ideas. Overcome the fear of trying something new and go for it. I will guarantee this; you won't be bored jumping out of a plane at 8,000 feet.

DISCOVER YOUR GOD-GIVEN PURPOSE

A person of purpose is less likely to fall into boredom and loneliness. When a person doesn't know where he or she is headed, idleness can take over, allowing too much time to think about self and all the negative things about life. Ephesians 5:15-16 in the Amplified Bible says, "Live purposefully and make the very most of your time!" If you do not know God's purpose for your life, set your mind now to passionately pursue Him to discover what it is. There are whole books dedicated to helping you find your purpose in life, but this book is not one of them. I just want to encourage you to make a decision to pursue God and discover His purpose for your life! The pursuit alone will bring fulfillment and help conquer loneliness.

GET YOUR EYES OFF SELF AND DO SOMETHING FOR SOMEONE ELSE

Most of the time when someone is feeling lonely and sad, it is when he or she is thinking only about "self." Look for opportunities to help a neighbor or someone you know who is in need of assistance. Maybe you could call a friend to encourage her with kind words. Maybe you could help a friend clean or decorate his home. Chances are, a single mom in your church or neighborhood would love to get out of the house with some of her friends, but she needs a babysitter. Guys, are there any ladies or elderly people who need their lawns mowed? The possibilities are endless.

One day a couple of friends broke down and finally told me what they thought of my couch. I thought the blanket I used to cover the rips looked quite nice, but these two women had a more accurate assessment. They decided to help me shop for a new couch and some home furnishings. We had a blast, especially the women. They thought it was great throwing things in the cart knowing it wasn't their money being spent! When we got back to my house, we discovered we were locked out. Now, if I had been alone, Lord knows how frustrated and angry I would have been. But, I wasn't. I was with friends, and we were having so much fun we just laughed.

When you do things for others, the biblical principle of sowing and reaping comes into effect. When you plant seeds of encouragement in the lives of others, God sees to it that others encourage you in return. This helps solve the loneliness in your own life. I have found that when I am doing something for someone else, it gets my mind off *me* and helps me leave loneliness alone.

I'm not pretending that developing friends, attending church, and having a hobby will fill the same needs that marriage does. Marriage will eventually happen, but committing your singleness to the Lord and practicing these keys will definitely help you overcome loneliness and enter a God-given rest.

What I have suggested so far are all external things you can do to help overcome loneliness. However, if you do not take care of the *internal self*, you will be lonely for the rest of your life regardless of your marital status or how many friends or hobbies you have.

If loneliness is indeed the problem, then the keys we have discussed will help solve it. But if you still feel lonely after doing these things, then we must consider the possibility that what you are going through is not loneliness, but perhaps sadness, due to an unmet desire. A person can have a hundred friends and still be sad. But it's important to realize that marriage is not the ultimate cure for sadness or loneliness. There are thousands of married people who experience great depths of sadness and are very lonely.

Jesus is the only cure for sadness. When a person is in love with Jesus and living life for the Lord, there is little room for the sadness that comes from loneliness.

I know it sounds simple, but it is the best advice I can give one experiencing loneliness: Fall in love with Jesus and develop an intimate relationship with Him. Practice Thank-You Prayers to get your mind off self and onto God. From there, start doing practical things like those you have read about in this chapter. Commit your life and the idea of being alone to the Lord. Leave loneliness alone and create a world around you of purpose, fun activities, friends, hobbies, and acts of kindness. You will find yourself leaving loneliness behind and enjoying life to greater degrees.

> Father, thank You for giving me ideas on how to overcome boredom and loneliness. I commit my singleness to You and choose to leave loneliness alone. Thank You for giving me Your rest. Thank You for drawing me closer to You and filling any gap in my heart that is causing sadness. Fill me with Your love and give me the confidence to meet new people and develop friendships. Finally, thank You, Lord, that I am actually never alone. You are with me wherever I go. I love You.

DISCUSSION QUESTIONS

1. Have you ever had a boyfriend/girlfriend? What were the results?

2. Are you in a dating relationship right now?

    Do you have a knowing in your heart that it is headed for marriage? If your answer is "no" or "I do not know," what are you going to do about it?

    Have you ever fasted the relationship to help ensure a more clear understanding of God's will about the relationship?

    If not, are you willing to follow this piece of advice in an effort to hear and obey God's voice concerning the relationship?

3. Are you ready to "Wait to date your mate"? What adjustments will you have to make to your thinking in order to raise this standard?

4. Are you lonely? What are you going to do about it? (How about getting a few friends to read this book with you?)

Section VI

Are You in Your Garden?

Chapter Thirteen

Being in the Right Place at the Right Time

"The steps of a man are established by the LORD;
And He delights in his way."
PSALM 37:23 (NAS)

    One of life's greatest keys is found in Psalm 37:23. Let's look at it in the Amplified Bible: "The steps of a [good] man are directed *and* established by the Lord when He delights in his way [and He busies Himself with his every step]." A good man is someone who walks in continual obedience to the Lord. When you live a life of obedience, God directs your steps. With God directing your steps, you will always be in the right place at the right time. Not just for meeting your future mate, but you will be at the right place for other divine opportunities as well.

    Through obedience to God, you will be at the right place to meet the person who will give you the job you need. Maybe you will happen to overhear a conversation that gives you the exact piece of wisdom you were seeking. The scenarios are endless. Life is not real life anyway, unless you are obeying God and living in His perfect will.

Remember the Garden of Eden? The Garden of Eden can represent God's perfect will. God brought Eve to Adam—in the garden. All provision needed to live a happy life to its fullest was in the garden.

If you choose to look outside of God's will for your life's partner, all you will probably find is someone else outside of God's will. You need to ask yourself, "Am I in my Garden of Eden? Am I in God's will for my life? Am I where God wants me to be?" When you can say yes to those questions, then you will be able to trust God with your future, including meeting your future mate.

Examine your life. Are you living in sin? Are you attending the church God has called you to attend? Are you running from God in your career decisions? Are you following the map of the Holy Spirit or the map of an unrenewed mind?

When you walk in obedience to God and obey the small promptings of the Holy Spirit, you remain in your "garden." As a result, you will be in the right places at the right times. Men, God will bring you your Eve. Ladies, God will take you to your Adam.

This reminds me of the day my wife, Pippa, and I met. I was at a Bible college in Dallas for ministry purposes with a man I'll call Bob, my senior minister. I was Bob's assistant, and he was scheduled to teach at the college for a week.

One day, I was watching a teaching video in the guest minister's apartment on campus. Bob walked in and asked me if I would go with him to the library. I told him, "I'd rather not go right now. Besides, it's raining."

About five minutes later, Bob came back and said, "Come on, Jeff. Don't you want to go over to the library just for a short time?"

Barely turning my head, I replied, "Not really. It's raining cats and dogs and I'm in the middle of watching this video. You can go if you want, but I think I'll stay here."

Once he left the room the second time, the Holy Spirit reminded me of Elijah and Elisha. I could hear Elisha telling

Elijah, "I will stay at your side until you die. I will not let you go alone, for God has called me to serve you." I started feeling convicted. Elisha would not leave Elijah's side even when Elijah told him to leave him alone. But me? I wouldn't even go to the library with the man I was called to serve. I decided to cut a deal with God. (Don't laugh. You've probably done the same thing before.) I said, "All right God, if Bob asks me to go over to the library one more time, I will say yes."

A moment later, Bob came back to the room saying, "It will only be a minute. How about you and I go across the street to the library?"

Trying to hide my frustration, I said, "All right, let's go." I started the process of attitude adjustment. Have you ever been there? I said, "OK, where are the umbrellas?" But, there weren't *umbrellas*, only one umbrella. You have to imagine this with me. I am 6 feet 6 inches tall. Bob is about 5 feet 10 inches. I'm the associate, so I get to hold the umbrella— primarily over Bob's head.

We take off walking briskly across the street with the umbrella over his head and me getting sopping wet. "I hope you're seeing this, God," I silently screamed. "Shining up another jewel for my crown! Amen."

We finally arrived at the library, and I was doing my best to accept my lot in life. After five minutes of drip-drying, I asked Bob, "Found your book yet? I think it's time to go." Of course, it wasn't even close to the time to go and he continued to browse.

Five minutes later, "OK, it looks like you found your book. Ready now?"

He shook his head, "Not now."

Then it happened. Out of the corner of my left eye, I saw the glass doors to the library open. A cloud of glorious smoke entered the room. From the midst thereof came the most gorgeous woman I have ever seen. This angelic being began to float, I mean walk, to the copy machine about twenty-five feet from where I was standing. Instantly, I knew there was something different about that woman. Before I had time to think, I found myself walking toward the copy machine.

An inward conversation erupted: "Jeff, what are you doing? *I don't know what I'm doing.* What are you going to say when you get there? *I don't know what I am going to say.*" And then, I found myself standing behind the young woman at the copy machine.

Approaching a woman was truly unlike me, and that fact caused me to ask myself what in the world I was doing. I decided I'd better say something or she might think I was standing in line for the copy machine. The problem was, I had no "opening lines" in my repertoire. But suddenly, just like that, the most incredible idea came to me. (Guys get your highlighter out, this was my pick-up line, and it worked.)

I tapped her on the shoulder and inquired, "Are you the tour guide?" (What? 'Are you the tour guide?' What kind of question is that? She's making copies. What does that have to do with giving tours?) But at the time, I was so proud of myself. I thought, "Yeah, that sounded pretty good." It seemed to roll off my tongue like poetry.

She looked up at me with a confused, but very cute, look on her face and said, "No."

Then I was stuck. For a moment I thought, "Now what do I do? Well, better stick with this tour guide theme or she may think I'm just trying to pick her up."

"You see that classroom over there?" I asked in my ever-so-suave manner. "What do they do in that room?"

"They have classes in that room," she answered.

"Ah, okay, what do they do in that room over there?" I keenly responded.

"They have classes in that room, too."

It was a disaster! (Goes to show how if God is putting two people together, it does not matter much what pick-up line the guy uses. God has a way of orchestrating His will in spite of our foolishness.) So, somehow, by the grace of God, she agreed to step into the foyer to continue our highly stimulating and intellectual conversation. The rest is history. After talking with Pippa for a short while, I knew I needed to spend more time with her.

It worked out for us to do so that week and from there, we developed a godly relationship and eventually got married.

Oh, by the way, Bob came out about ten minutes later and said, "OK, I'm ready to go now."

To which I responded, "Go? Hey what's the hurry? Don't you want to check out another book?"

What is the point of this story? To dangle in your face the fact that I am married? Absolutely not! I want to emphasize the point of how vital it is to walk in continual obedience to God. You never know what you will find one day in your garden. Your day will come. When God directs your steps, you will be in the right place at the right time to meet the right people, including your future mate.

You may be thinking, "What if you had not gone to the library that day?" I believe the answer to that question is found somewhere in Isaiah 55:8-9:

> "For My thoughts *are* not your thoughts,
> Nor *are* your ways My ways," says the LORD.
> For *as* the heavens are higher than the earth,
> So are My ways higher than your ways,
> And My thoughts than your thoughts.

No one knows how God orchestrates our destinies. Pippa and I would probably have met at some other time. Do not try to figure God out; just trust and obey. When you do, you will find yourself in the right places at the right times.

Once you meet the man or woman of your dreams, the journey is not over. When you start to develop that special relationship, you enter what I call the Passion Zone. Passion between two people headed for marriage adds a whole new dimension to the journey. If you think you needed God's grace before you met Mr. or Miss Right, welcome to the next level! It's after you've met this person that you really need God's help!

CHAPTER FOURTEEN

Passion and Purity

"There's something mystic about lips; given enough time, they always seem to find each other."

The movie is finished and there you are alone in the car with your date.

"What do you want to do now?"

"I don't know. What do *you* want to do?"

"I don't care. What do *you* want to do?"

Back and forth it goes. Finally, the man of the relationship suggests praying together. After a few moments of prayer, he then quotes the Scripture, "If two shall agree on earth as *touching*, they shall have what they ask." So he suggests holding hands, for agreement purposes of course, and before you know it, your "praying in agreement" session turns into a "getting too close" session. There's something mystic about lips; given enough time, they always seem to find each other.

One of the strongest forces of nature is our passion for and attraction to the opposite sex. God created something beautiful

111

when He created the physical intimacy between a man and a woman. This passion is a vital element to a rich marriage; however, it proves to be one of the greatest challenges on the journey *to* marriage. God created us with this sex drive, but if not controlled, what was created for good can be used of the enemy to bring pain and destruction. The Lord's plan and desire is for this passion to be fulfilled. However, in order to walk in its highest fulfillment, we must follow God's Word.

Have you heard the phrase, "I burn for you"? The idea is not new. Proverbs 6 compares sex to fire. Both have been created by God and serve a wonderful purpose when inside His plan.

The fireplace in my living room is used to build fires that heat the whole room. You can even roast marshmallows there if you want. But the fire is great only as long as it stays in the fireplace. There's no need to tell you what would happen if I took a burning log out of the fireplace and placed it on my couch. The same thing is true with sex. God created sex and has given it a wonderful purpose in life. But, just like fire, sex has its place, and that place is called marriage. Marriage is to sex what the fireplace is to fire. When fire gets outside the fireplace, we have problems; when we get involved with sex outside of divine boundaries, we have problems.

The world says as long as two people are in love or consent, it is okay to have sex. This philosophy is one of the biggest lies Christians are falling for every day. Sex is not for two people who are in love. Sex is for two people who are MARRIED. Any sexual conduct outside of marriage is sin and will bring the same results as taking fire out of the fireplace. If you want to learn more on the results of sexual behavior outside of marriage, just read Proverbs 5, 6, and 7. These chapters are full of the consequences of ungodly sexual relations and give you keys on how to stay pure.

"So, what do you do with the passion until you are married?" you ask.

You control it. One of the earmarks of a man or woman of God is the ability to control fleshly impulses. The way they do this is with wisdom, the Word of God, and Thank-You Prayers.

The first step to controlling passion and remaining pure can be summed up in one word—avoid. Proverbs 4:15, speaking of the path of temptation, says, "Avoid it, do not go on it; Turn from it and pass on." This means avoid images and words that bring impure thoughts. Avoid compromising situations and positions. Avoid date boredom or unplanned activities with the opposite sex. Avoid a vacation mentality. The problem is that most people put themselves in compromising positions of romantic temptation and wonder why they have difficulty staying pure. The solution is to avoid.

When thoughts leading to temptation arise, get your mind on things that are pure with Thank-You Prayers:

> Father, thank You for helping me avoid this temptation. Thank You that I have self-control and with Your grace I think only pure thoughts.

The struggle starts with your thought life, and your thoughts are what make you who you are. Proverbs 23:7a says, "For as he thinks in his heart, so *is* he."

Once a young man came to me and told me he had a problem with lust and controlling himself around women. I asked him what kind of movies he watched, what kind of music he listened to, and what kind of magazines he read. Not surprisingly, all of them involved sexual content. I told him he did not have a lust problem; he had a *head* problem.

You cannot fill your life with things of the world and expect to act like Jesus. What you see and hear will create images and thoughts that will directly influence your desires and eventually your actions. When you see and hear ungodly things, seeds are planted on the soil of your heart and mind. Eventually those seeds will produce a harvest of sinful impulses and, ultimately, sinful acts. The same is true when you see or hear godly things like the Word of God. The words that fall on your heart are seeds that eventually bring a divine harvest.

Thank-You Prayers can help you keep a pure thought life. When tempted to think impure thoughts or watch something ungodly, turn the temptation into a Thank-You Prayer:

> Father, thank You for giving me grace to think on good things. Give me grace to not watch ungodly things. I turn my attention to You and choose to keep a pure heart.

It helps even more if you actually say your prayer out loud. There is power in the spoken Word of God.

Beyond what you see and hear, you need to be careful where you go. You need to avoid situations of temptation. Avoid being alone for lengthy periods of time in a car or house with someone to whom you are attracted. Plan your date night, leaving no room for "down time." During down times couples get bored, and boredom is the breeding ground for sin. If you are in a relationship headed for marriage and staying pure is proving difficult, make sure you have your dates planned. Women, before you go out with your boyfriend, ask what he has planned. If he does not know, wait till he does. If you are already out and there is nothing planned for the rest of the evening, have him take you home and drop you off—don't invite him inside.

You may think this sounds square. It certainly is perceived that way from the world's perspective. However, wouldn't you rather avoid painful pitfalls than experience emotional hurt in an attempt to be accepted by our present society's loose standards?

Women, beware of a man who says, "I love you with all my heart, and if you really loved me then you would have sex with me." The truth is, a person who truly loves you will not want to put you in a position of paying the consequences of the sin of fornication. Someone who really loves you wants you to remain pure and walk in righteousness. Thank-You Prayers come in handy when faced with sexual temptation.

> Thank You, Jesus, for giving me grace to control myself. Thank You for giving me wisdom in what I can do to avoid situations of compromise. Thank You for helping me honor You in all I do.

Realistically, we can often make this part of life more difficult for ourselves. We defy wisdom and put ourselves in compromising situations. Then, when a lustful thought enters our mind, we unwisely entertain it. I have heard it said about temptation, "You can't help it when a bird flies over your head, but you can surely stop it from nesting in your hair!" The key is to actively swoosh away temptation as soon as it flies into your mind. Better yet, stay away from places where you know such "birds" usually fly!

Controlling yourself is not easy; in fact, it's a battle. This is why Ephesians 6 tells us to put on the whole armor of God. It does not say put on your bathing suit and hit the beach for a vacation. It does not say sit in the Jacuzzi with your date and expect your flesh to behave. You have to take up the sword of the Spirit and tenaciously fight temptation in prayer and deed.

Secondly, to control passion and stay pure, pump yourself full of the Word of God. Psalms 119:9 and 11 says,

> How can a young man cleanse his way?
> By taking heed according to Your word.
> Your word I have hidden in my heart,
> That I might not sin against You!

Thirdly, you need to realize that as a Christian, the same Spirit that raised Christ from the dead dwells in you (Romans 8:11). If the Holy Spirit has the power to raise Christ from the dead, He can surely give you the power to overcome temptation.

> Father, thank You that Your Word is working mightily in me both to will and to do Your good pleasure. My strength is in You. Thank You for the power of the Holy Spirit working in me to help me control my passions and live a holy life in honor of You.

The real issue is not about fornication—it is about honoring the Lord. First Corinthians 10:31b says, "Whatever you do, do all to the glory of God." We all must commit to honoring God and giving Him glory in every area of our lives. Receiving the grace to control passion and stay pure begins with a decision to bow your life to God in humility.

> God, I confess I have fallen short of Your will in my relationships. Thank You for Your forgiveness. Now I ask You to give me grace to change my lifestyle. I will pursue You and Your Word with more passion. With Your help, I commit to practice purity in every area of my life.

Let's stop looking for a magical cure that allows us to flirt with sex without sinning. Let's avoid images and thoughts of sex outside of marriage. Let's embrace God's thoughts, and live a righteous life. Use wisdom, fill your life with the Word of God, yield to the Holy Spirit, practice Thank-You Prayers, and you will find that staying pure in your relationships is not as difficult as you once thought.

Your obedience to God's call to holiness will produce great benefits. And some of the best rewards for staying pure while you are single will only be realized on your honeymoon and in the days and years beyond.

Thank You, Jesus, for grace to live a pure life. Help me rid my life and home from all sources of temptation. Thank You for forgiveness from past failures, and the grace and wisdom to avoid future ones. You are my passion! You are my life!

Chapter Fifteen

Secret Petitions

*"Delight yourself in the LORD;
And He will give you the desires of your heart."*
PSALM 37:4 (NAS)

This is one of the most famous Scriptures in the Bible. I especially appreciate how the Amplified version puts it: "Delight yourself also in the Lord, and He will give you the desires *and* secret petitions of your heart." So, what does it mean to delight yourself in the Lord? What exactly are secret petitions, and how do they relate to being single? You're about to discover the answers to those questions.

God is such a loving God; He is always looking for opportunities to bless His children. One of the best ways God shows His love is by granting secret petitions. When I was in high school, I used to lie awake at night listening to Leon Patillo on my now extinct record player. My favorite was his live album on which he sang the song, "You Are Flesh of My Flesh." As I drifted off to sleep, I would ponder on how nice it would be to have that song sung at my wedding. I never told a soul; only Jesus knew. It was a secret petition.

A secret petition could be a desire only you and Jesus know about. God takes pleasure in giving us our desires and what the *Amplified Bible* calls "secret petitions." However, God does not want to give us our desires outside of an intimate fellowship with Him. For this reason, the verse first says we must delight ourselves in the Lord.

The word *delight* is an interesting word. In the original Hebrew language, it means "to be soft and pliable." When I first discovered this in *Strong's Concordance*, I was confused. How does delighting myself in the Lord relate to being soft and pliable? As I sought the Lord, He reminded me of when I was totally in love, or perhaps infatuated, with my college girlfriend. Whatever this girl wanted me to do, I did.

"You need me to wash your car? Okay."

"You want me to walk you to class? Sure."

"Can I carry your books? Great!"

I was willing to do anything for this girl. I was so in love! One night after curfew at Oral Roberts University, she called to tell me she was craving pizza. At 1:30 in the morning, she couldn't go get one or have one delivered, so she called to ask me to do it. There was a pizza joint in the area that stayed open late for the foolish and indulging, so I gave them a call and ordered her favorite kind. The dormitory was locked and I couldn't bring the pizza to her door—university rules. But love would not be thwarted. My maiden in distress lowered a rope made out of belts from her third-floor window and I tied it around the pizza box. I tied that knot with such loving, tender care!

A fool in love, you say? Most definitely. There I was, in the middle of the night, risking getting caught and severely disciplined just to meet the self-involved needs of my dearly beloved sweetheart. You laugh, but I know you too have done some pretty foolish things in the name of love. (I had an even greater love for my wife, Pippa, when we dated, but fortunately for me we lived in two different cities and I was nine years older. The distance, plus being more mature and wiser, helped me to contain myself a little better.)

I remember specifically what my college roommate said when I returned from delivering the pizza. "You're putty in that girl's hands," he told me. I did not want to admit it, but it was true. I was truly soft and pliable, just like putty. Is this what Psalm 37 is talking about when it says, "Delight yourself in the Lord"? I have discovered that's exactly what it means.

To delight yourself in the Lord means to be madly in love with Jesus to the point that you'll do anything for Him, even if it seems foolish. The thought of getting caught does not faze you a bit. Why? Because you're so in love. To *delight* means you are soft and pliable, like clay in the Potter's hands. If God tells you to do something, you do it with joy. If the Holy Spirit prompts you to do something in the middle of the night, you don't roll over and yawn. Instead, you get up with excitement, willing and ready to do whatever He asks.

Delighting in the Lord is allowing God to mold and shape you into the person He wants you to be, and loving every minute of it. Why do you love it? Because you know it's helping you get closer to Jesus and become more like Him.

God's greatest desire is to have a passionate love relationship with His children. When this intimacy with the Lord is developed, He begins to bring us our most desired dreams and even our secret petitions. God knows it's safe to grant those desires, because He knows your desires have been refined by His presence. He gets great joy in granting the desires of His loved ones.

Fifteen years after my times of lying in bed listening to Leon Patillo, I found myself planning a wedding with a beautiful woman named Pippa. She told me about all the songs she wanted to have sung at our glorious ceremony. I agreed, and told her it was her day to pick whatever songs she wanted. In all our discussions about the wedding, we never even mentioned a Leon Patillo song. Then rehearsal night came. Pippa had her brother sing one song, and a friend another. As I listened to them rehearse, I thought about the song I had always wanted to hear at my wedding, but I was determined not to put any pressure on Pippa by asking her to include a song she might think was corny. Then I began to reason: "Well, I never claimed it or declared it or confessed it three times a day. I didn't bind it, curse it, loose it, or even fast forty days for this to come to pass. I guess that's the way it is. No Leon song." I accepted it and moved on.

The next thing I knew it was our wedding day and Pippa was walking down the aisle in her gorgeous wedding gown. We lit candles, had communion, and everything else you do during the ceremony. One person sang a song, and the other person sang another. Then, after Pippa and I said our vows, her father, who conducted the wedding, handed my bride a cordless microphone. I got really nervous. "Hey, we didn't rehearse this," I thought. "What's going on here? Am I supposed to have a microphone, too?" I knew Pippa had never sung in public, so I expected her to perhaps recite something. But then the pianist struck a few notes and Pippa surprised me by singing me a song. Guess which song. That's right, "You Are Flesh of My Flesh" by Leon Patillo.

I was in shock. I could not believe it. Then it was as if I felt Jesus tapping me on the shoulder and whispering in my ear, "I heard your secret petition." I was overwhelmed that Pippa loved me enough to sing to me at our wedding. I was overwhelmed that she sang so well. And I was overwhelmed by the realization that God loved me so much He was granting my secret petition from fifteen years ago.

God hears secret petitions and He is sensitive to strong desires. But does this mean we will receive *every* desire we have secretly prayed for? No, but the desires God knows are best for us will be granted. He even knows the desires you may not yet be aware of. One desire, that may be a secret to you, lies in the deepest corridors of every Christian's heart. It is the desire to know Christ and to be in His presence.

When you lay your head on your pillow, tell Jesus how much you love Him. Spend time with the Lord in prayer expressing your heart to Him. Let Him know how much you need Him and depend on Him for everything in life. When you do this, your love relationship with Jesus will grow.

Delight yourself in the Lord, and He *will* give you the desires and secret petitions of your heart. Fall wholeheartedly in love with Jesus. Place your life in His hands; be soft and pliable. The next time the Holy Spirit asks you to do something, ask yourself if you are in love with Jesus enough to do it. If you are, you will find fulfilled secret petitions popping up all throughout your life.

I have shared this personal story with you to give you hope. God is with you. He sees your heart's desires. As you delight yourself in the Lord, He will bring you your secret petitions. However, in the meantime, enjoying where He has you now can be a challenge. You can do it! Apply the principles you learn in this book and you will be able to enjoy the journey.

> Jesus, I delight myself in You. I love You more than I will ever love anyone here on earth. I give my life to You as clay in the Potter's hands. Help me be soft and pliable so You can mold me into the person You want me to be. As I delight myself in You, thank You for bringing me the secret petitions of my heart.

DISCUSSION QUESTIONS

1. Are you in your garden? Are you in God's will for your life? If not, what steps of obedience do you need to take to get there? What has God been prompting you to do?

2. Are you living a pure life? If you have sin in your life, put this book down now, and confess your sin to God. Receive His forgiveness according to 1 John 1:9.

3. What do you need to specifically avoid to help you stay pure? Places? People? Things? Internet? Discuss and write down three things that you are going to either throw away or set guards against to avoid.

4. Do you have any secret petitions? If you feel comfortable in sharing one of them, do so now. (Telling someone a secret petition does not exclude it from the promise of God bringing it to pass.)

5. Do you have a story about how God brought you one of your secret petitions?

6. In private, write down a few secret petitions. One day you may turn to this page and rejoice in how much God loves you.

Section VII
Forgiveness, Freedom, and Healing

*"When he falls, he shall not be hurled headlong;
Because the L*ORD *is the One who holds his hand."*
PSALM **37:24 (**NAS**)**

Chapter Sixteen

Is That You, God?

"I have freed you from your past."
—God

Receiving secret petitions is great. However, most people experience hurt and pain along the way. I was working in the reference library at Oral Roberts University at the time my college girlfriend and I broke up. My job was to sit at a desk in the library and check out reference materials. I did not get much business during the day; I usually just did homework. (Don't tell my boss.)

One day, shortly after that two-year relationship ended, I was flooded with horrible memories. I remembered every hurtful incident as if it just happened: I remembered the times she brought her roommate on our dates, the times she chose to go out with her friends instead of me, the gifts she accepted from other guys who liked her, even little things like the times she was late for important dates. It all seems silly now, but at the time, each hurt caused an intense emotional battle. I realize now that a lot of times my pain had nothing to do with something my girlfriend did or did not do; it was merely a result of my immaturity and insecurities. However, I did not see it that way back then.

On this day in the library, all the heartache I had suppressed rose to the surface. I was tormented! The devil told me I had made a huge mistake. "You wasted two years of your life," he whispered. "How could you let her do all those things to you? You should have ended the relationship a year ago. You were too weak to express your heart."

I took the devil's words and used them as a bat to beat myself up. Every word was another hammer blow to my soul. I think I had a glimpse of the beginning of a nervous breakdown. This was serious! I could not sit still. I squirmed in my chair, trying to shake off the thoughts of guilt, condemnation, and depression bombarding my mind. Back then, I did not recognize it as an attack. I thought it was just me remembering all the bad things she did to me. I sat there saying, "Jeff, shut up—stop thinking about that. It's over. Shut up. Think about something else." I kept on trying to tell myself, "It's not that bad; it's over."

Then I heard a voice. I thought someone was behind the bookshelves. I said, "Excuse me. Who's there?" I did not hear anything else, so I tried to focus on my work once more. Then I heard it again. I could not make out the words, but someone was definitely there. In fact, I was so sure that I got up and looked behind the shelves to see who it was. But no one was there. The reference room was empty.

Now I was perplexed. Who was saying those things? What was he saying? I thought one of my friends was playing a trick on me. I sat down and pondered what was happening. Then I turned my attention to the Lord and said, "Are you trying to tell me something?"

God answered. This time, it was not audible to my outward ear, but it was like a huge speaker inside my chest that said, "I have freed you from your past, and I am sending you My best." I will never forget those words. They carried an anointing to destroy the yoke of bondage that I was under as a result of my broken relationship—a relationship I had thought would last a lifetime.

I sheepishly whispered God's words out loud: "You have freed me from my past and You are bringing me Your best?"

Immediately the torment lifted and I felt like a free man. It was like someone had lifted heavy chains off my shoulders. It's hard to explain, but I know deep in my soul that this was an act of God. I was free! With a big smile on my face I repeated the words again, this time with confidence: "You have freed me from my past, and You are sending me Your best."

Just a simple phrase, but so awesomely powerful when spoken by God. All my supposed hurts came into perspective. I found myself able to forgive my ex-girlfriend and let go of my past. Whenever I thought of her or saw her, I learned to turn it into a Thank-You Prayer. God helped me walk in newfound freedom.

Have you gone through a hurtful relationship? If so, God is saying the same simple phrase to you right now. "I have freed you from your past, and I am bringing you My best."

Think of the people who have hurt you. Begin to thank God for giving you grace to release them into His hands. Speak each person's name out loud and proclaim him or her forgiven by you and by God. Every time you see that person say, "Father, thank You that I have forgiven that person. Thank You for freeing me from my past." Every time the devil reminds you of the hurtful things someone did to you, turn it into prayer: "Thank You, Father, for healing me. That person is forgiven and released into Your hands. I choose to bless that person."

Eventually, the mention of that person's name or the memory of any person who has done you harm will no longer carry with it the power to depress or hurt you. God takes the sting out of bad memories. He heals the brokenhearted.

No Christian should be walking in bondage or fear of his or her past. God is God of the past, present, and future. No matter how dark your past, God washes it white as snow. There is nothing in your past that God cannot cleanse. If you can trust Him with your future, you can trust Him with your past. If you can give Him your future, you can give Him your past. Jesus shed His blood to wipe away the load of guilt and condemnation we carry due to our mistakes and failures. He took stripes on His back and died on the cross to heal the wounds that come from mistakes and life's hardships. There is nowhere you hurt that God cannot heal. There is nothing broken that God cannot fix.

Your future is not dictated by your past; your future is dictated by what you believe God says about you. And He says you are forgiven. He says you are set free. He says you are a winner in His eyes. The more you see yourself as God sees you, the more you will walk in the liberty He has provided for you. The key is forgiveness. Forgive and release those who have hurt you, and allow God to heal your heart.

Unforgiveness in your heart puts you in bondage. I heard one preacher say that unforgiveness is the only prison you can be in that the guard throws you the key and says, "You can leave anytime you want to." How do you leave? You take the key of forgiveness and use it!

> Thank You, Father, for the ability to forgive. Thank You that whom the Son has set free is free indeed! Thank You for helping me continue to release the past and walk in total forgiveness. Thank You, Jesus, for healing my heart and giving me true freedom.

Chapter Seventeen

Look in the Mirror; What Do You See?

"You are valuable and precious."
—Jesus

Jennifer responded to my altar call for releasing the past and receiving inner healing. When I started to pray for her, the Lord gave me a vision of heaven. I saw Jesus lifting His left hand, looking at a huge diamond ring on His finger. He was in pure delight as He gazed upon the beautiful stone. He could not contain His excitement. Jesus turned to God and said, "Look, Father, isn't it beautiful?"

As God turned, a bright light hit the diamond and caused a million rays of light to shoot in every direction.

"Wow!" Jesus said. "Isn't it spectacular?"

"Yes," said the Father, "it is the most beautiful diamond I have ever seen."

Jesus stood up and began to twirl around like a new bride enraptured by her wedding ring. The glorious light beaming through the atmosphere caught the attention of the angels.

Amid the worship of "Holy, Holy, Holy," you could hear the angels *oohing* and *ahhing* as they pointed at the ring and whispered to each other.

"Isn't it beautiful?" Jesus asked the cloud of witnesses who were already stunned with amazement. You could tell He was proud of His ring and its obvious beauty.

"It's one of a kind!" an angel shouted.

"It's so bright that I can hardly look at it," another bellowed.

"It's priceless," two angels concluded after trying to calculate the value of such a precious stone.

Jesus made His way back to the throne. "Look, Father, look. Isn't it the most precious thing You have ever seen?"

"It certainly is," God firmly agreed. "It certainly is."

Then, in the vision, Jesus looked at me and said, "Whisper in Jennifer's ear and tell her, 'You're that diamond on the ring finger of Jesus.'"

Jennifer was already in tears as I told her the story. But, when she heard those words of Jesus, her whole body went limp. She began to cry uncontrollably. God was supernaturally ministering to her, freeing her from her past and healing her from her deep-seated pain. She had endured some painful relationships that had caused her to doubt her sense of worth. For years, she had silently battled thoughts of insecurity and low self-esteem.

Can you relate to Jennifer? Countless people are riddled with hurt, pain, and confusion due to abuse and broken relationships—including relationships with parents. If you are one of those who have gone through several painful relationships, you most likely have battled thoughts of low self-esteem. If you have been repeatedly told that you will never amount to anything or been asked, "Why can't you be more like your brother or sister," you probably struggle with low confidence and a poor self-image.

Sometimes a *lack* of words can be just as detrimental as hurtful spoken words. If a woman has rarely heard "I love you" from her father, or a man has never heard "I'm proud of you, son," they both will struggle with insecurities and self-doubt. These insecurities are perpetuated and deepened by every broken relationship.

Each word we hear paints another brush stroke on the canvas of our hearts that holds the picture of how we see ourselves. Faith is the brush we can use to paint God's image of ourselves on our heart. Unfortunately, doubt is a brush within arm's length as well. The brush of doubt is used to paint a negative picture. Words and thoughts are on the palette we dab our brush on and bring to the canvas of our heart. We paint our own self-image. And, we have the power to choose which brush to pick up and what paints to use.

I waited while Jennifer wept, responding to the anointing that she was experiencing. Deep wounds were being healed, as if God was erasing the picture she had painted on her heart and was replacing it with a whole new, priceless *Master*piece.

Then the Lord gave me a word of wisdom. "Jennifer, when you go home tonight, go into the bathroom and shut the door. Look into the mirror and say these words to yourself, 'You are beautiful. You are precious. You are valuable. You are the diamond on the ring finger of Jesus.'" I encouraged her to do this at least three times a day.

This powerful word of wisdom was not sent just for Jennifer. If you relate to her in any way, this word is now being sent to you, too. In fact, over the years, God has reminded me of this vision on a number of occasions while I have been ministering to people. Amazing results have occurred each time God has prompted me to share this message with a group or individual.

A couple years ago, I gave a message called "How to be a Dream Achiever" to a group of youth leaders. At the end of the lesson, God moved in a powerful way and people wept for thirty minutes. While the Lord was ministering to people, He reminded me of the vision of heaven and the words of wisdom to Jennifer. Once the weeping settled down, I shared the vision with the entire group. Some began to weep again, while others looked at me with big smiles, as if they had just gotten saved. It is a powerful vision from God and I encourage you to take it for yourself. What you will be doing is changing the picture on your heart of how you see yourself. This is not mind over matter; it is having faith in what God says about you.

Practice picking up the brush of faith, and by agreeing with God's words, paint a biblical picture of who you really are in Christ. See yourself as God sees you by thinking and saying things about yourself that God thinks and says about you. In the next chapter, you will find a list of Scriptures to get you started. Every time you look at yourself in the mirror and say what God says about you, you're that much closer to seeing His intended masterpiece of who you really are.

The first time you go to the mirror, you may not be able to look yourself in the eye and say the things I've encouraged you to say. That's fine. Begin by saying the words out loud. Keep working at it until you can boldly look yourself in the eye and say, "You are valuable. You are beautiful. You are precious. You are the diamond on the ring finger of Jesus." Your confidence in the Lord will grow each time you do.

Jennifer's life was changed that day. How deep and long-lasting the change will be is up to her and her consistency in applying the wisdom of God. The same is true for you. I hope you apply this word to your own life and begin painting a whole new picture of yourself on the inside. Having a good picture of yourself on the canvas of your heart is vital to enjoying life and becoming all that God has called you to be. How you see yourself eventually turns into how others see you and treat you.

Decide right now to see yourself through God's eyes. Paint a positive, biblical picture on your heart of who you are. When thoughts of poor self-image creep back, throw down the brush of doubt and pick up the brush of faith by speaking what God says about you in a Thank-You Prayer.

Thank You, Jesus, that I see myself as You see me—valuable and precious. Thank You, Lord, for helping me paint a good picture of myself that portrays what You say about me. Thank You that my past is behind me and together we are going forward enjoying the masterpiece You are developing in my heart.

When the past knocks on your door trying to present your old picture, slam the door and begin to thank God for the new picture He is helping you create. Take a moment right now to think: How do you see yourself? Is the vision of Jesus and the ring a word of wisdom for you? If so, put the book down right now and find a mirror. Your life will never be the same.

Discussion Questions

1. Is there anyone you need to forgive? What are their names?

Pray a prayer of forgiveness:

Dear God, I choose to forgive _____ right now. I release him/her now into Your hands and cancel any debt I think they owe me for what he or she did to me. Whenever I think of that person, give me grace to say, Thank You Jesus, I have forgiven that person. My heart is free from pain!

2. Have you ever gone through a painful relationship? Do you still feel the effects in your heart? No matter how hard your heart hurts, God can heal you and release you from your past. Pray this prayer:

> Dear God, I come to You in Jesus' name asking You to heal my heart. I forgive those who have hurt me. I ask for Your healing anointing to flow through me right now, binding up my wounds, and restoring my soul to wholeness. I release my past and put it under the blood of Jesus. I declare I am free. I declare I am healed. My future is not dictated by my past; my future is dictated by what I believe You say about me. Because of You, Jesus, my future is bright. Thank You for healing me.

3. Do you have a healthy, godly self-image? We all have some insecurities as a result of hearing and believing wrong things. Discuss and write down a list of Bible-based prayers that you can say when you look yourself in the mirror. You can use the "I am" list in the next chapter to get you started. Memorize two or three statements and declare them throughout the day.

Section VIII
Single Again

Chapter Eighteen

I Thought for Sure I'd Never Be Single Again

"I will never leave you nor forsake you."
—God

Sarah's heart sank as she pulled into the shopping-center parking lot. It was her first time dropping off the children to spend the weekend with their dad since the divorce. She couldn't help it; a fear of being alone overwhelmed her. The divorce happened so fast, now things seemed to be going in slow motion. Sarah never thought she'd be in this situation: Is this really happening to me?

Roger comes home from work and sits in his driveway trying to muster up the strength to go inside. He knows no one will be there. No wife, no kids, just him. As he opens the front door a sense of loneliness seizes his heart when no children run to him yelling, "Daddy's home!" The stillness is paralyzing. There's the family photo hanging in the foyer. His son's fishing rod, that he's been meaning to fix, is leaning against the wall. Then, there's his own room. Roger's heart aches as he thinks: God, I don't know if

I can do this. I don't know if I am going to be able to go on. After eight years of marriage, Roger finds himself alone. "What do I do now?" he asks himself. "I never thought I would be single again."

Multitudes of people find themselves single again, even after many years of marriage. The scenarios are too numerous to mention.

Some would say that being single after marriage is more difficult than never being married at all. However, the circumstances that lead to distraught emotions are not as important as the emotions themselves.

A trap some people fall into is the thinking that their problem is somehow unique; they are the only one experiencing such pain and confusion. Ordinary keys don't apply to them because they have extra ordinary problems.

The truth is, there is only one Bible, just like there is only one true God. There is not a big Bible for big problems and a small Bible for small problems. God's principles and wisdom for successful living are the same regardless of how hurt, confused, stressed, depressed, or frustrated you are. "But Jeff, you have no idea what I've been through." You're right, and don't take this wrong, but I don't need to know what led up to, caused, or perpetrated your emotional state. It doesn't change God's Word on how to overcome and live in peace.

Remember Philippians 4:6-7? It says be anxious for nothing, but in *every circumstance*, pray with thanksgiving…and God's peace will keep your heart and mind fixed on Christ. The principle of Thank-You Prayers laid out in this book apply to any situation in life, including being single after marriage. However, I realize there are some additional challenges a once-married single may face.

MEMORIES—GOOD AND BAD

Memories can rob you of your present joy and happiness. Of course there are the bad memories, but what about the good? Unlike a single that has never been married, you have to deal with the memory of *getting* married. You have the photo album reminding you of your intimate times and the vows that were spoken to you. You may be living in the same house, sleeping in the same bed, eating at the same dinner table that used to be shared with your spouse. Most likely there are the fond memories of having your first child and how excited you and your spouse were when he took his first step.

What do you do when memories try to throw you into an emotional gloom? How do you guard yourself from longing for the past and thinking, *If only it could be like it used to be?* You do the same thing the never-been-married single does when he or she longs for the future—you turn your anxiety into peace with Thank-You Prayers.

> Thank You, Jesus, for taking the sting out of my memories and only allowing me to experience joy when I think of my past. Thank You that my past will not dictate my future, but I choose to put it behind me and press on.

DASHED HOPES AND DREAMS

Not only are there memories of the past, but what about the dreams of the future? You were already on your way to fulfilling a dream with your spouse. Maybe you were in business together or even in full-time ministry. Now what? You can't fulfill the dream on your own...*or can you?*

Joshua was Moses' right-hand man for years. They were both going to go into the Promised Land and enjoy God's provision as a big happy family. Then Moses died and left Joshua holding the reigns of the dream. When faced with the impossible, God told Joshua:

> Have I not commanded you? Be strong and of good courage; do not be afraid, nor be dismayed, for the LORD your God *is* with you wherever you go. (Joshua 1:9)

Don't give up on your dreams and visions! When you picture yourself in the future, you will be tempted to see yourself alone. But wait, *God is with you wherever you go.* Don't say, "Well, when I look into the future, my spouse is not there, so I guess I can't fulfill my dreams." Your ex-spouse may have taken the car, house, or even the kids, but he or she can never take your potential! Yes, your life has changed and you may have to adjust your dreams. But, with God, all things are possible!

RIPPING OF DEEP INTIMATE HEART TIES

The longer a couple is harmoniously married, the deeper the emotional ties. How God connects two people's hearts is part of the mystery of marriage. Though the principles of God's power to heal apply to any level of pain, I understand some hurts go deeper than others. Someone who has experienced a divorce or even a loss of a spouse will have to continue to apply the washing of God's Word for a period of time in order to enjoy complete freedom. Don't give up. There is no pain that God cannot utterly heal.

Every time your heart hurts, don't ignore it, push it down, or just give it time. Time alone does not heal, it just buries. God says that He sent His Word to heal. Sometimes the memory is not removed, but God can take away the sting and heal the negative results associated with the memory. Open your heart to the Lord and express your desires to Him in scriptural Thank-You Prayers. Each time you do, you will be applying healing balm to the wound. *Then*, over time you will experience complete healing.

FEAR OF BEING ALONE

I talked with a woman who was recently divorced. She expressed attacks of intense fear—the fear of being alone. A person who is thirty-five and never married should be quite used to the idea of coming home to an empty home, eating meals alone, and sleeping alone. (Better be sleeping alone!) But, what if you have been coming home to a spouse for the last twenty years and now there's only the cat?

Unfamiliar with the Singles' Scene

Do I sit with all the single people in church? Do I go to the singles' Sunday School? Where do I fit in? Do I have to go out on dates? These are all questions a newly divorced person may ask. I say, take your time. Focus on your healing and growing intimate with Jesus.

In the beginning, it is difficult for divorced people to even admit to *themselves* they are divorced, let alone speak freely about it to others. People need to learn to give room to recently divorced or widowed singles. Don't pressure them into quickly fulfilling their new single role. Give them time. Pray for and support them. Allow God to minister to them and meet their needs.

Single Parenting and Dealing with the Ex

Unlike a boyfriend and girlfriend breaking up after two years of dating, most people who have been married have children. Every scenario is different, but there are visitation agreements, alimony, and child support issues that will probably last for many years. Many ex-spouses never arrive at a friendly relationship. Dealing with each other can prove to be very stressful, including the continuation of hurtful words and jabbing remarks. You may have an ex-spouse who lies, corrupts your children, and uses them to get back at you. I have not spoken to my ex-girlfriend from college in over fifteen years. Get the point?

What do you do when you are single again?

What do you do when you find yourself single and in a position that you thought you would never be in again? In addition to practicing Thank-You Prayers and applying the wisdom in this book, here are a few keys:

Turn to God and Reestablish Your Intimacy with Jesus

Overcome the temptation to turn to another human to meet your needs or see you through this difficult time. Friends can help support you, but no human can satisfy your soul, heal your heart, or fill the void left through a broken marriage or loss of a spouse. Only God can do that. Pursue Jesus like never before! Saturate your soul with God's Word and His presence. Listen to good teaching tapes, godly music, and read good books. In *His* presence there is fullness of joy.

God says if we seek Him, He'll take care of us.

> The young lions lack and suffer hunger;
> But those who seek the LORD shall not
> lack any good thing. (Psalm 34:10)

I know a woman whose husband had an affair. Instead of using it as an excuse to backslide, go after the guy who had been flirting with her, or isolate herself, she pressed into God. She stayed under the covering of her local church pastors and searched for Christian books relating to her situation. She probably read twenty books in six months. God has seen her through.

Recommit Jesus as Lord of your life and keep Him in control. Don't allow your ex to determine your decisions. *Well, she's got a new boyfriend, so I am going to go out and get me a new partner, too.* You do what is right, regardless of his or her actions. Jesus will see *you* through, too.

Work Through Forgiveness

Don't allow what your ex-spouse did or said to you ruin the rest of your life by carrying unforgiveness. Holding a grudge, stonewalling, or keeping unforgiveness in your heart is like preparing a vial of poison for *them*, but drinking it *yourself*. You must release your spouse to God and cancel any debt you feel he or she owes you. (See "Is That You God?")

Many times a divorce is filled with angry and hurtful words. Be sure to not allow the words of an angry ex determine how you see yourself. (See "Look in the Mirror, What Do You See?") Pray for God to protect your heart from the seeds of those words and keep scriptural Thank-You Prayers in your mouth. No matter what your ex-spouse has said, you are valuable and precious in God's eyes.

On the other hand, take responsibility for your own faults that contributed to the broken relationship, even if your angry spouse pointed them out to you. Listen to what was said and do not allow *how* it was said to excuse you from honest self-evaluation. Many times people don't mean what they say when angry, but sometimes things said in anger are right on target. Ask God to help you discern. If for the past two years of your marriage your spouse said you were controlling…look into it. Take it to God and ask Him to reveal things that need change.

PURSUE FRIENDSHIPS WITH PEOPLE OF THE SAME SEX

Women, beware! Guys love women crying on their shoulders. There are lots of men who would love to comfort you in your despair, but their motives may not be pure. The same warning goes for the men. There's no shortage of women that would love to hear your heart and share your pain.

Anyone who has gone through a broken relationship is very vulnerable to the embrace of the opposite sex. And that can lead to even more pain. I advise for a period of time to develop relationships solely with the same sex. Keep in mind that this is secondary to developing your relationship with Jesus.

Finally, let it go. Do not allow your past or your marital status define who you are or where you are going. In 1 Corinthians 7:17, The Message Bible says, "God, not your marital status, defines your life."

Ask God how He wants to use you in this season of life and don't use divorce as an excuse to not get involved in church. You have a bright future. Life is not over. You are loved, accepted, cherished, wanted, and needed by God and others.

Let the principles in this book directly apply to you. Scriptural Thank-You Prayers will help you live in peace and reach your potential in God regardless of your circumstances.

DISCUSSION QUESTIONS

1. Did you ever think you would be single again? Every situation is different, but if you are single again, what has been your most difficult challenge and how has this chapter helped you?

2. Have you been able to release the past? What is still lingering in your soul? What do you think needs to take place in order for you to be completely free from the effects of your past?

3. If you have never been married, has this chapter helped you better understand a person who has been through a broken marriage or has lost a spouse? Explain how.

4. If you are single again and reading this book in a group with singles who have never been married, what advice could you give them from your perspective? What would you like singles who have never been married know, to better understand someone who has gone through a divorce or loss of a spouse?

Section IX
Final Thoughts

*You will never be perfect,
nor will you find the perfect mate,
but you can strive for excellence
and be the best you can be.*

Chapter Nineteen

A Little Friendly Advice

*"Listen to counsel and receive instruction,
That you may be wise in your latter days."*
Proverbs 19:20

The second part of Proverbs 21:11, in the *Amplified Bible*, says, "Men [and women] of godly wisdom and of good sense learn by being instructed." So, for this final chapter, I thought I would leave you with a little friendly advice. This advice is not exhaustive by any means, just a few good ideas to help you during your single years and beyond.

Be Yourself

There is nothing worse than trying to impress people with a false image out of fear that they may not like the real you. This is not just unrewarding but also exhausting. When you meet someone, be yourself. If you do not like to jog, don't say *yes* to jogging just because you think this new acquaintance may not like you otherwise. If you are always being yourself, you won't have the strain of trying to remember what kind of image you have portrayed to each person you have met. There are no roles to memorize or personality traits to remember. You can relax and just be what comes natural to you—you! Let's face it, when you are getting to know someone, you want to be shown the real person, not some false image. So, give that person the same respect and let him or her get to know the real you.

DEVELOP CONFIDENCE

You will be more apt to be yourself when you have confidence. The reason people display false images is because they are not happy with their true identity. If you develop confidence in yourself based on who you are in Jesus, you will be free to be yourself. There are volumes written to help people discover who they are in Christ and how to develop confidence. This is not one of those volumes; however, I will say a few things that may help.

We can do or be nothing without Christ; we can do and be all things *through* Christ (John 15:5, Philippians 4:13). The key is growing in the knowledge of who the Bible says you are in Christ and realizing that you are here to please God, not man.

One way to develop confidence is to read the Bible and declare it out loud. Find Scriptures that talk about who you are in Christ and speak them out loud to yourself. This is not magic or the power of positive thinking. Faith comes by hearing the Word of God (Romans 10:17). It is faith that paints a good picture of yourself and convinces your soul of the truth of God's Word. The Bible is full of Scriptures stating who you are in Christ. Here are a few:

I AM...
- **a child of God** . . . . .Romans 8:16
- **redeemed from the hand of the enemy** . . .Psalm 107:2
- **forgiven** . . . . .Colossians 1:13-14
- **justified** . . . . .Romans 5:1
- **sanctified** . . . . .1 Corinthians 6:11

a new creature . . . . .2 Corinthians 5:17
partaker of His divine nature . . . . .2 Peter 1:4
redeemed from the curse of the law . . . .Galatians 3:13
delivered from the powers of darkness .Colossians 1:13
kept in safety wherever I go . . . . .Psalm 91:11
strong in the Lord and in the power
    of His might . . . . .Ephesians 6:10
able to do all things through Christ . . .Philippians 4:13
an heir of God and a joint heir with Jesus Romans 8:17
blessed coming in and going out . . .Deuteronomy 28:6
blessed with all spiritual blessings . . . . . .Ephesians 1:3
healed by His stripes . . . . .1 Peter 2:24
above only and not beneath . . . . . . .Deuteronomy 28:13
more than a conqueror . . . . .Romans 8:37
not moved by what I see . . . . .2 Corinthians 4:18
walking by faith and not by sight . . . .2 Corinthians 5:7
being transformed by the renewing
    of my mind .Romans 12:1-2
the righteousness of God in Christ .2 Corinthians 5:21
an imitator of Jesus . . . . .Ephesians 5:1
the light of the world . . . . .Matthew 5:14
overcoming by the blood of the Lamb
    and the word of my testimony . . . .Revelation 12:11

What do you think would happen if you chose to agree with God's Word and said these things out loud in faith, every day? One thing is for sure; you would develop confidence. Consistency is the key. Don't just read this list once and forget about it. Memorize a few and declare them out loud every day—throughout the day.

Many times a person's level of confidence can be detected in the first minute of conversation. It always saddens me when I meet a young man with little confidence. He comes up to me, lightly shakes my hand and does not look me in the eye. Brothers, can I give you some advice? When meeting someone, walk up to him or her with confidence. Look that person in the eye and say, "My name is _____. What's yours?" When shaking a person's hand, give it a firm grip, with moderation. (The tightness of the squeeze does not necessarily indicate the level of manliness.) Just do not give it a wimpy, barely hold-on type of grip. You might want to practice this with a friend. Remember, eye contact and firm grip.

Confidence is something that grows over time. However, be cautious to never allow your confidence to be in the flesh. This breeds arrogance and pride. Always remember, if not for Christ, you would be nothing.

BE PROACTIVE

You need to be proactive in meeting new people and developing relationships. Instead of sitting around, call someone and invite him or her over to your home. "Well, brother Jeff, she has never invited me over to *her* house?" That's probably what she's thinking. Be the mature one and make the call.

Do not do what I did for most of my single years. I would go to church, and because I lacked confidence, I would sit in the back and leave right after the preaching. It is hard to meet new people that way, let alone develop any kind of relationship. It was only when I was coerced into going to a church retreat that I met some people who became my good friends.

Organize a cookout at your home. Put an announcement in the church bulletin that all the singles are gathering at Billy Bob's Pizza after Sunday night service. I used to organize card parties. We would sit up late at night laughing and playing and just having a good time.

Another thing you can do is invite a friend or two to special events: concerts, plays, church or singles' retreats, white-water rafting, hiking, theme parks, water parks, museums, and whatever else that is available in your area. The key is being proactive. You organize or search out local events. You call the people. You put the announcement in the bulletin.

Keep Yourself Clean

It's a good idea to shower every day. This also includes brushing your teeth and even carrying mints. Body odor and bad breath are not conducive to making a good first impression or developing relationships. In case you haven't discovered this yet, your breath can be offensive shortly after brushing your teeth. That's where mints come in handy.

Remember the day I met Pippa at the copy machine? Imagine if I had eaten a foot-long hotdog with onions right before I went to the library that day. I would have walked up to Pippa, leaned over and said, "Hello. Are you the tour guide?" She would have taken two steps back and possibly fainted. Upon coming to, she probably would not have wanted to continue our conversation. There is nothing wrong with eating foot-longs with all the extras; just brush your teeth afterward and carry mints.

Look Your Best

It is a good idea to dress well and keep your outward appearance presentable. This does not mean you have to wear an evening gown or three-piece suit everywhere you go, but wherever you do go, try to look decent. Dressing sloppily with your hair in a mess will probably dampen your social life. (Keep smiling! Remember, this is just friendly advice.)

I hope you are catching what I am trying to get at here. Of course the inside of a person's heart is what really counts, but our outward appearance is part of the package when we meet people and develop relationships.

"Jeff, I want to marry a sharp businessman. One who loves the Lord with all his heart. But I don't seem to meet anyone like that."

Well, it might have something to do with the nose ring and five earrings you wear. Or, maybe the fact that you wear pants three sizes too big that hang halfway down your hips and you wear black makeup and sit in the back row.

I know I am being a little facetious, but I hope you get my point. I'm not saying any particular type of apparel is wrong or sinful, but how you dress does say a lot about who you are. Maybe you are a man who wears a shirt and tie everywhere you go, even to the grocery store. Nothing wrong with that; it just adds to how others define who you are.

BE CAREFUL WITH WHOM YOU ASSOCIATE

Many times people have an impression about us before they even know our names. They get that impression from seeing who we associate with. If you see someone hanging around people who do not love Jesus, you naturally assume that he or she also does not love Jesus. So the crowd you associate with helps others define who you are. And in a very real way, it *is* who you are. The advice is this: Be yourself, but know that who you associate with greatly determines what kind of people you are going to meet and what impression people initially have of you. I call it the impression before the first impression.

KEEP YOUR EYES ON JESUS

This, of course, is good advice in any season of life. We all need to keep our eyes on Jesus, especially when we are waiting for a desire to come true. We need to remember Jesus is our reason for living. When we have our eyes on Him, we are able to enjoy life to its fullest. When we focus on what we do not have or what we think is negative, we tend to get depressed. As Psalm 37 says, "Delight yourself also in the Lord."

To sum up, looking for a mate is not about finding the right one as much as *being* the right one. Examine yourself to see if there is anything you can do to improve yourself and be more like Jesus. You will never be perfect, nor will you find a perfect mate, but you can strive for excellence and be the best you can be. Ultimately, we need to be ourselves and keep striving to become more like Christ. Trying to be something we are not will only lead to insecurity and confusion.

When you discover something about yourself that needs to change, ask God to help you and do your best to improve. If you cannot find anything about yourself that needs improvement, look harder or ask a close friend. As long as you are still on earth, there's plenty of room for positive change. You just have to humble yourself and be honest.

Freedom comes from being content with who you are. However, it should be every Christian's goal to become more like Christ. In order for Christ to be your goal, you must have your eyes on Him.

PRAY FOR YOUR FUTURE MATE

Chances are your future mate is alive right now. (At least I hope so, especially for those of you in your twenties and beyond.) So, why not start praying for him or her today? Ask God to protect and lead him or her in His perfect will. Think of what kind of prayers you would like your future mate to pray for you. Turn those prayers around and start praying similar prayers for him or her. Your prayers will go before you and actually help you discern God's will for your relationship when you do meet. There's power in prayer.

One could add a hundred items to this list of simple advice—that's why we have the Bible. Colossians 2:3 tells us that all the treasures of wisdom are hidden in Jesus. Make a quality decision to consistently read the Bible, seek God's face, and develop an intimate relationship with Jesus. God will help you through your journeys of life. Remember, we are all on this same journey—the journey of becoming more like Christ. Choose to enjoy every step of the way!

DISCUSSION QUESTIONS

1. What piece of friendly advice do you need to take to heart?

2. When you close your eyes and ask God for advice, what does He say? Discuss and write down three things God is prompting you to change about your life.

Now do them, and you will be blessed!

> But he who looks into the perfect law of liberty and continues *in it*, and is not a forgetful hearer but a doer of the word, this one will be blessed in what he does. (James 1:25)

Section X
Scriptural Prayers

"Do not fret or have any anxiety about anything, but in every circumstance and *in everything, by prayer and petition (definite requests), with thanksgiving, continue to make your wants known to God. And God's peace [shall be yours, that tranquil state of a soul assured of its salvation through Christ, and so fearing nothing from God and being content with its earthly lot of whatever sort that is, that peace] which transcends all understanding shall garrison and mount guard over your hearts and minds in Christ Jesus."*

PHILIPPIANS 4:6-7 (AMP)

CHAPTER TWENTY

Thank-You Prayers

*Thank You, Jesus, because of You and Your grace,
I have the ability to have peace and enjoy life.*

This section of the book is full of scriptural prayers you can pray throughout your single journey. It is a powerful tool to help you keep your eyes on the Lord. Some of the prayers you will read in the next section are prayers I personally prayed for years. I would have enjoyed having a book like this when I was single. I encourage you to carry this book with you, or put it where you can read it and refer to it on a regular basis. Let it not only be a source of encouragement, let it serve as a tool and reminder to practice the principle of Thank-You Prayers every day of your life.

The following are categories of different temptations and struggles that cause stress, confusion, frustration, and anger in a single's life. Pray these prayers as often as the situations knock on the door of your heart. Don't just read these prayers over and over again; let them become a part of you. Through the power of these Thank-You Prayers, and others you develop on you own, you'll be able to enjoy every journey of life!

CATEGORIES

- Why Am I Still Single? 163
- When Is It Going to be My Turn? 165
- HELP! My Best Friend Is Getting Married 167
- I Thought for Sure I'd Never Be Single Again 168
- Wisdom and Discernment 171
- Insecurities and a Lack of Confidence 176
- I Just Got Dumped 178
- Healing from the Past 183
- The Unknown Future 186
- Purity 189
- Depression 191
- Loneliness 194
- Discouragement 195
- Receiving Forgiveness 196
- Giving Forgiveness 199
- Your Future Mate 200
- Closing Prayer 201

Enjoy your peace-filled journey!

Why Am I Still Single?

For my thoughts are not your thoughts, neither are your ways my ways, saith the LORD. For as the heavens are higher than the earth, so are my ways higher than your ways, and my thoughts than your thoughts.
—Isaiah 55:8-9 (KJV)

Trust in the LORD with all thine heart; and lean not unto thine own understanding. In all thy ways acknowledge him, and he shall direct thy paths.
—Proverbs 3:5-6 (KJV)

Father, I thank You that Your thoughts and ways are higher than mine. I do not understand why I am still single, but I trust You with all my heart. Thank You for directing my paths.

For in Him we live and move and have our being, as also some of your own poets have said, "For we are also His offspring."
—Acts 17:28

Thank You, Lord, that I am Your child, and regardless of any circumstance, in this I will rejoice! I choose to count my blessings and be thankful for what I have. You are my reason for living. In You do I live, move and have my being.

Therefore humble yourselves under the mighty hand of God, that He may exalt you in due time, casting all your care upon Him, for He cares for you.
—1 Peter 5:6-8

Lord, I humble myself under Your mighty hand. I cast the whole idea of still being single onto You. Thank You, Jesus, for caring for me. Thank You for using this time to develop me into a wonderful person for my future mate.

> Draw near to God and He will draw near to you.
> —James 4:8a

> Peace I leave with you, My peace I give to you; not as the world gives do I give to you. Let not your heart be troubled, neither let it be afraid.
> —John 14:27

Thank You, Jesus, for the gift of peace; I choose not to let my heart be troubled. Thank You for enveloping me with Your love during this season of my life and always. I choose to draw closer to You; thank You for drawing closer to me.

> If any of you lacks wisdom, let him ask of God, who gives to all liberally and without reproach, and it will be given to him.
> —James 1:5

> However, when He, the Spirit of truth, has come, He will guide you into all truth.
> —John 16:13a

Thank You for the Holy Spirit leading me and guiding me into all truth. Lord, give me wisdom and show me areas of my life that need to change. Thank You for helping me develop into a man/woman of God.

When Is It Going to be My Turn?

Rest in the LORD, and wait patiently for him: fret not thyself because of him who prospereth in his way.
—PSALM 37:7A (KJV)

Wait on the Lord: be of good courage, and he shall strengthen thine heart: wait, I say, on the Lord.
—PSALM 27:14 (KJV)

Thank You, Jesus, for giving me rest in You. Thank You for giving me courage and strengthening my heart as I live my life for You. I patiently wait upon You knowing my future is in Your hands.

Delight thyself also in the LORD; and he shall give thee the desires of thine heart. Commit thy way unto the LORD; trust also in him; and he shall bring it to pass.
—PSALM 37:4-5 (KJV)

Let your conduct *be* without covetousness; *be* content with such things as you have.
—HEBREWS 13:5A

Father, I desire to get married. Thank You that as I have my eyes and affection on You, You shall give me the desires of my heart according to Your will. I commit the whole idea of marriage to You, and trust that You shall bring it to pass. In the meantime, I choose to be content in You.

The steps of a good man are ordered by the LORD: and he delighteth in his way.
—PSALM 37:23 (KJV)

> But the fruit of the Spirit is love, joy, peace, longsuffering, kindness, goodness, faithfulness, gentleness, self-control. Against such there is no law.
> —Galatians 5:22-23

Thank You, Lord, that my steps are ordered of You and, in Your timing, You will bring me my mate. Thank You that I have the fruit of the Spirit, and You are helping me develop patience.

> But as for me, I trust in You, O Lord;
> I say, "You are my God."
> My times are in Your hand.
> —Psalm 31:14-15a

> Be still, and know that I *am* God.
> —Psalm 46:10

Thank You, Jesus, my future and all it holds is in Your hands. Thank You that I can trust You. I will wait patiently for You and Your timing. I will be still and know You are God.

> Roll your works upon the Lord [commit and trust them wholly to Him; He will cause your thoughts to become agreeable to His will, and] so shall your plans be established *and* succeed.
> —Proverbs 16:3 (AMP)

Father, I roll my life and my desire to be married upon You and trust You with all my heart. I thank You that, as I do this, You will cause my thoughts to become agreeable to Your will and my plans to get married will succeed according to Your will.

HELP! MY BEST FRIEND IS GETTING MARRIED.

To every thing there is a season, and a time to every purpose under the heaven.
—ECCLESIASTES 3:1 (KJV)

Rest in the LORD, and wait patiently for him: fret not thyself because of him who prospereth in his way.
—PSALM 37:7A (KJV)

Let your conduct *be* without covetousness; *be* content with such things as you have. For He Himself has said, *"I will never leave you nor forsake you."*
—HEBREWS 13:5

Thank You, Jesus, I can get excited about my best friend's wedding. Bless him/her with a great marriage. Thank You that my turn is coming, and my friends will be excited for me, too. Thank You for giving me grace to be content as I wait patiently on You and Your timing.

I Thought for Sure I'd Never Be Single Again

> For I know the thoughts that I think toward you, says the Lord, thoughts of peace and not of evil, to give you a future and a hope. Then you will call upon Me and go and pray to Me, and I will listen to you. And you will seek Me and find *Me*, when you search for Me with all your heart. I will be found by you, says the Lord.
> —Jeremiah 29:11-14a

Thank You, Jesus, my life is not over. You have great plans for me! Thank You for hearing me when I cry out to You. I will seek You with my whole heart. Thank You for letting me find You!

> Do not fear, for you will not be ashamed;
> Neither be disgraced, for you will not be put to shame;
> For you will forget the shame of your youth,
> And will not remember the reproach of your
>   widowhood anymore.
> For your Maker is your husband,
> The Lord of hosts is His name;
> And your Redeemer is the Holy One of Israel;
> He is called the God of the whole earth.
> —Isaiah 54:4-5

Thank You, Jesus, I do not have to fear being ashamed. Thank You for helping me release any feeling of disgrace and remember it no more. Thank You for being my spouse and redeeming me from any negative effects of what I have gone through.

The Lord is my shepherd;
I shall not want.
He makes me to lie down in green pastures;
He leads me beside the still waters.
He restores my soul;
He leads me in the paths of righteousness
For His name's sake.
Yea, though I walk through the valley of the
    shadow of death,
I will fear no evil;
For You are with me;

—Psalm 23:1-4

But now, thus says the Lord, who created you,
    O Jacob,
And He who formed you, O Israel:
"Fear not, for I have redeemed you;
I have called you by your name;
You are Mine.
When you pass through the waters, I will be with you;
And through the rivers, they shall not overflow you.
When you walk through the fire, you shall not
    be burned,
Nor shall the flame scorch you.
For I am the Lord your God,
The Holy One of Israel, your Savior;

—Isaiah 43:1-3a

Father, because I have made You Lord of my life, You are my Shepherd. Thank You for providing my every need, including peace and comfort. Even though I feel like I am walking in the deepest valley of my life, thank You that I do not have to be afraid. Thank You that no matter what I go through, I am Yours and You are with me.

This is my comfort in my affliction,
For Your word has given me life.
—Psalm 119:50

For I will turn their mourning to joy,
Will comfort them,
And make them rejoice rather than sorrow.
—Jeremiah 31:13b

O Lord my God, I cried out to You,
And You healed me.
—Psalm 30:2

He heals the brokenhearted
And binds up their wounds.
—Psalm 147:3

Thank You, Jesus, for Your Word that gives me life. Thank You for comforting me and turning my mourning into joy. I receive Your healing power. Thank You for taking away my sorrow and binding up my wounds. I choose to rejoice in You.

O you afflicted one,
Tossed with tempest, and not comforted,
Behold, I will lay your stones with colorful gems,
And lay your foundations with sapphires.
I will make your pinnacles of rubies,
Your gates of crystal,
And all your walls of precious stones.
All your children shall be taught by the Lord,
And great shall be the peace of your children.
—Isaiah 54:11-13

Thank You, Jesus, You are rebuilding my life on a beautiful foundation. Thank You that my children will grow up in peace because You are their teacher.

> You will show me the path of life;
> In Your presence *is* fullness of joy;
> At Your right hand *are* pleasures forevermore.
> —Psalm 16:11

> Looking unto Jesus, the author and finisher of *our* faith
> —Hebrews 12:2a

Thank You, Jesus, that *You* will show me the path of life and how to live as a single person again. I will not turn to another besides You because it is only in *Your* presence that I will find fulfilling joy.

Wisdom and Discernment

> The fear of the Lord *is* the beginning of wisdom,
> And the knowledge of the Holy One *is* understanding.
> —Proverbs 9:10

Lord, I bow my heart to You in reverence. Thank You for giving me wisdom in every area of my life. Thank You for developing the fear of God in my life.

> When wisdom enters your heart,
> And knowledge is pleasant to your soul,
> Discretion will preserve you;
> Understanding will keep you,
> To deliver you from the way of evil,
> From the man who speaks perverse things.
> —PROVERBS 2:10-12

Father, thank You that Your wisdom will keep me from making wrong decisions in relationships. As I grow in Your wisdom, I thank You that it will keep me from the way of evil and the path of wicked people. Thank You that Your wisdom is pleasant to my soul.

> And when he brings out his own sheep, he goes before them; and the sheep follow him, for they know his voice. Yet they will by no means follow a stranger, but will flee from him, for they do not know the voice of strangers.
> —JOHN 10:4-5

> For this reason we also, since the day we heard it, do not cease to pray for you, and to ask that you may be filled with the knowledge of His will in all wisdom and spiritual understanding; that you may have a walk worthy of the Lord, fully pleasing *Him*, being fruitful in every good work and increasing in the knowledge of God.
> —COLOSSIANS 1:9-10

> But there is a God in heaven who reveals secrets.
> —DANIEL 2:28A

Thank You, Jesus, I hear Your voice, and no other voice do I follow. Thank You for filling me with all wisdom and spiritual understanding. Thank You for revealing Your will for my relationships and in all areas of my life. My future is no secret to You; thank You for revealing it to me in Your timing.

> If any of you lacks wisdom, let him ask of God, who gives to all liberally and without reproach, and it will be given to him.
> —JAMES 1:5

> For "who has known the mind of the LORD that he may instruct Him?" But we have the mind of Christ.
> —1 CORINTHIANS 2:16

> If you seek her as silver,
> And search for her as for hidden treasures;
> Then you will understand the fear of the LORD,
> And find the knowledge of God.
> For the LORD gives wisdom;
> From His mouth come knowledge and
>   understanding;
> He stores up sound wisdom for the upright;
> He is a shield to those who walk uprightly;
> He guards the paths of justice,
> And preserves the way of His saints.
> Then you will understand righteousness *and* justice,
> Equity and every good path.
> —PROVERBS 2:4-9

Father, I seek and ask for wisdom in Jesus' name. Thank You for giving me the mind of Christ and helping me make right choices in relationships. Help me understand the fear of God so I may walk in Your wisdom.

> That the God of our Lord Jesus Christ, the Father of glory, may give to you the spirit of wisdom and revelation in the knowledge of Him.
> —Ephesians 1:17

> The teaching of the wise is a fountain of life, that one may avoid the snares of death.
> —Proverbs 13:14 (AMP)

Thank You, Jesus, that I have the Spirit of wisdom and every decision I make is influenced by Him. Thank You that with Your wisdom I will avoid the pitfalls in life, including destructive relationships.

> Her ways are ways of pleasantness, and all her paths are peace.
> —Proverbs 3:17 (KJV)

> And let the peace (soul harmony which comes) from Christ rule (act as umpire continually) in your hearts [deciding and settling with finality all questions that arise in your minds, in that peaceful state] to which as [members of Christ's] one body you were also called [to live]. And be thankful (appreciative). [giving praise to God always].
> —Colossians 3:15 (AMP)

Thank You, Jesus, that I know Your ways. I let Your peace be the umpire for all my decisions. Thank You, Jesus, that I am able to discern between good and bad relationships. Thank You for increasing Your peace when I am on the right path and removing Your peace if I should go astray.

> However, when He, the Spirit of truth, has come, He will guide you into all truth; for He will not speak on His own *authority*, but whatever He hears He will speak; and He will tell you things to come.
> —JOHN 16:13

Thank You, Jesus, that I have the Holy Spirit, and He is guiding me into all truth. Thank You, with the help of the Holy Spirit, I will never be deceived by a man or woman or fall into a deceptive relationship.

> Where *there* is no counsel, the people fall;
> But in the multitude of counselors there is safety.
> —PROVERBS 11:14

Thank You, Jesus, for surrounding me with wise friends and counselors who are not afraid to speak the truth in love in order to help me stay on the path of righteousness. Give me grace to hear what You are saying through them.

> But, speaking the truth in love, may grow up in all things into Him who is the head—Christ.
> —EPHESIANS 4:15

> There is no fear in love; but perfect love casts out fear, because fear involves torment. But he who fears has not been made perfect in love.
> —1 JOHN 4:18

Thank You, Jesus, for friends that love me enough to overcome fear and speak the truth to me even when the truth hurts. Thank You for giving me grace to be that kind of friend so we can all grow up in Christ.

INSECURITIES AND A LACK OF CONFIDENCE

> For we are His workmanship, created in Christ Jesus for good works, which God prepared beforehand that we should walk in them.
> —EPHESIANS 2:10

> The LORD will perfect *that which* concerns me;
> Your mercy, O Lord, *endures* forever.
> Do not forsake the works of Your hands.
> —PSALM 138:8

> In whom we have boldness and access with confidence through faith in Him. Therefore I ask that you do not lose heart at my tribulations for you, which is your glory.
> —EPHESIANS 3:12-13

Thank You, Father, I am Your workmanship created in Christ Jesus. You not only made me but You are working in me continually to perfect that which concerns me. Because of You, I have bold confidence in every area of life.

Being confident of this very thing, that He who has begun a good work in you will complete *it* until the day of Jesus Christ.

—PHILIPPIANS 1:6

For it is God who works in you both to will and to do for *His* good pleasure.

—PHILIPPIANS 2:13

Thank You, Jesus, for the confidence in knowing what You have begun in me You are faithful to complete. Thank You that You are all the while working in me both to will and to do Your good pleasure.

I have strength for all things in Christ Who empowers me [I am ready for anything and equal to anything through Him Who infuses inner strength into me; I am self-sufficient in Christ's sufficiency].

—PHILIPPIANS 4:13 (AMP)

Thank You, Father, for infusing me with Your inner strength. Thank You that I am ready for and equal to anything that comes my way for I can do all things through Christ who strengthens me.

For God has not given us a spirit of fear, but of power and of love and of a sound mind.

—2 TIMOTHY 1:7

Thank You, Father, that I have nothing to fear for You have given me a spirit of love, power, and a sound mind. Thank You, Lord, that I can walk in confidence knowing who I am in Christ.

I Just Got Dumped

> The LORD your God is with you, he is mighty to save. He will take great delight in you, he will quiet you with his love, he will rejoice over you with singing.
> —Zephaniah 3:17 (NIV)

Father, thank You that You are with me right now, and You are well capable of helping me in this time of hurt. Thank You that no matter what anyone else thinks or says, You take great delight in me. Thank You for quieting me with Your love.

> Let us therefore come boldly to the throne of grace, that we may obtain mercy and find grace to help in time of need.
> —Hebrews 4:16

Father, I ask for Your grace now, in Jesus' name. Thank You for filling me with Your grace, Your ability beyond my own, to go through any circumstance in life.

> Hast thou not known? hast thou not heard, that the everlasting God, the LORD, the Creator of the ends of the earth, fainteth not, neither is weary? there is no searching of his understanding.
> He giveth power to the faint; and to them that have no might he increaseth strength. Even the youths shall faint and be weary, and the young men shall utterly fall:
> But they that wait upon the LORD shall renew their strength; they shall mount up with wings as eagles; they shall run, and not be weary; and they shall walk, and not faint.
> —ISAIAH 40:28-31 (KJV)

Father, even though You are an awesome God who never grows weary, I thank You for understanding me and accepting me in my weakness. I thank You that as I wait on You, You shall renew my strength and mount me up with wings as eagles to soar above this difficult time in my life.

> O keep my soul, and deliver me: let me not be ashamed; for I put my trust in thee. Let integrity and uprightness preserve me; for I wait on thee.
> —PSALM 25:20 (KJV)

Thank You, Jesus, for guarding my heart and not letting me be ashamed. I choose to trust in You and keep my integrity no matter what I am going through.

Finally, all of you, live in harmony with one another; be sympathetic, love as brothers, be compassionate and humble. Do not repay evil with evil or insult with insult, but with blessing, because to this you were called so that you may inherit a blessing. For, "Whoever would love life and see good days must keep his tongue from evil and his lips from deceitful speech."
—1 Peter 3:8-10 (NIV)

If it is possible, as much as depends on you, live peaceably with all men. Beloved, do not avenge yourselves, but *rather* give place to wrath; for it is written, *"Vengeance is Mine, I will repay,"* says the Lord. Do not be overcome by evil, but overcome evil with good.
—Romans 12:18-19,21

Do not say, "I will do to him just as he has done to me; I will render to the man according to his work."
—Proverbs 24:29

But I say to you, love your enemies, bless those who curse you, do good to those who hate you, and pray for those who spitefully use you and persecute you.
—Matthew 5:44

Father, thank You for giving me grace to love, be compassionate and humble. With Your grace, I choose not to repay insult with insult, but I choose to bless others and overcome evil with good. I pray blessings over the people who hurt me. Thank You for blessing me according to Your Word.

To comfort all that mourn; To appoint unto them that mourn in Zion, to give unto them beauty for ashes, the oil of joy for mourning, the garment of praise for the spirit of heaviness; that they might be called trees of righteousness, the planting of the LORD, that he might be glorified.

—Isaiah 61:2b-3 (kjv)

Weeping may endure for a night, but joy cometh in the morning.

—Psalm 30:5b (kjv)

Thank You, Jesus, for comforting me. Thank You for taking away this spirit of heaviness and replacing it with a garment of praise. Thank You that I am beautiful in Your sight, and You are filling me with Your joy.

Let no corrupt word proceed out of your mouth, but what is good for necessary edification, that it may impart grace to the hearers. And do not grieve the Holy Spirit of God, by whom you were sealed for the day of redemption. Let all bitterness, wrath, anger, clamor, and evil speaking be put away from you, with all malice. And be kind to one another, tenderhearted, forgiving one another, just as God in Christ forgave you.

—Ephesians 4:29-32

Cease from anger, and forsake wrath;
Do not fret, *it leads* only to evildoing.

—Psalm 37:8 (nas)

Father, with Your grace, I choose to forgive and let go of any anger or bitterness. Help me be kind and tenderhearted regardless of my circumstances.

> *Let your* conduct *be* without covetousness; *be* content with such things as you have. For He Himself has said, "I will never leave you nor forsake you."
> —HEBREWS 13:5

Jesus, You are my all in all. I will be content in You. Thank You for never leaving me. Knowing You are always by my side is the most comforting feeling on earth. I can always count on You.

> Now hope does not disappoint, because the love of God has been poured out in our hearts by the Holy Spirit who was given to us.
> —ROMANS 5:5

Thank You, Jesus, when my hope is set on You I will never be disappointed. Thank You for pouring Your love into my heart. Because I have Your love, I lack nothing.

> Do not sorrow, for the joy of the LORD is your strength.
> —NEHEMIAH 8:10B

Thank You, Jesus, for filling my heart with Your joy and giving me strength. I choose to walk in that joy and enjoy my life with You.

Be merciful unto me, O God, be merciful unto me: for my soul trusteth in thee: yea, in the shadow of thy wings will I make my refuge, until these calamities be overpast.

I will cry unto God most high; unto God that performeth all things for me. He shall send from heaven, and save from the reproach of him that would swallow me up. Selah. God shall send forth his mercy and his truth.

My soul is among lions: and I lie even among them that are set on fire, even the sons of men, whose teeth are spears and arrows, and their tongue a sharp sword. Be thou exalted, O God, above the heavens; let thy glory be above all the earth. My heart is fixed, O God, my heart is fixed: I will sing and give praise.

Awake up, my glory; awake, psaltery and harp: I myself will awake early. I will praise thee, O LORD, among the people: I will sing unto thee among the nations.

—PSALM 57:1-5, 7-9 (KJV)

Thank You, Jesus, I can run to You in times of trouble and hide under Your wings until difficult times pass. Even though I feel like I am being attacked, I choose to fix my eyes on You and exalt You with praise and worship. Thank You for keeping my heart steadfast through tough times.

HEALING FROM THE PAST

The LORD has appeared of old to me, saying:
"Yes, I have loved you with an everlasting love;
Therefore with lovingkindness I have drawn you.
Again I will build you, and you shall be rebuilt."

—JEREMIAH 31:3-4A

Thank You, Jesus, for loving me so much that You draw me to You. Thank You for healing me and rebuilding anything broken in me with Your love.

> Therefore we also, since we are surrounded by so great a cloud of witnesses, let us lay aside every weight, and the sin which so easily ensnares *us*, and let us run with endurance the race that is set before us, looking unto Jesus, the author and finisher of *our* faith, who for the joy that was set before Him endured the cross, despising the shame, and has sat down at the right hand of the throne of God.
> —Hebrews 12:1-2

Thank You, Lord, for giving me grace to lay aside my past and not allow it to hinder me any longer. Thank You for setting me free to run the race with joy. With You as the author and finisher of my life, I can win any race.

> Surely He hath borne our griefs and carried our sorrows.
> —Isaiah 53:4a (kjv)

> I sought the Lord, and he heard me, and delivered me from all my fears. They looked unto him, and were lightened: and their faces were not ashamed.
> —Psalm 34:4-5 (kjv)

Thank You, Jesus, for bearing my grief and carrying my sorrows on the cross. Thank You for wiping away shame and delivering me from my fears. I look to You now for approval and acceptance.

> Brothers, I do not consider myself yet to have taken hold of it. But one thing I do: Forgetting what is behind and straining toward what is ahead, I press on toward the goal to win the prize for which God has called me heavenward in Christ Jesus.
> —PHILIPPIANS 3:13-14 (NIV)

I choose to put my past behind me and under the blood of Jesus. Thank You, Jesus, for helping me let go of my past and press on toward the future with You.

> Therefore, if anyone *is* in Christ, *he is* a new creation; old things have passed away; behold, all things have become new.
> —2 CORINTHIANS 5:17

Thank You, Lord, that I am a new creation in You. My old past has passed away, and You have caused all things to become new. Thank You for giving me a brand new image of myself in You.

> I waited patiently for the LORD; and he inclined unto me, and heard my cry. He brought me up also out of an horrible pit, out of the miry clay, and set my feet upon a rock, and established my goings.
> And he hath put a new song in my mouth, even praise unto our God: many shall see it, and fear, and shall trust in the Lord.
> —PSALM 40:1-3 (KJV)

Thank You, Jesus, for hearing my heart cry and rescuing me out of the pit. My feet are now set on a rock of stability. I will sing a new song to You and make a melody of praise in my heart. Thank You for establishing my steps. I trust You with my life!

The Unknown Future

> You will show me the path of life;
> In Your presence *is* fullness of joy;
> At Your right hand *are* pleasures forevermore.
> —Psalm 16:11

Thank You, Jesus, for showing me the path of life. I trust You to show me which way to turn every step of the journey. Thank You that Your path of life leads me to Your presence where I can be filled with joy and find pleasure.

> The LORD is my light and my salvation; whom shall I fear? the LORD is the strength of my life; of whom shall I be afraid?
> —Psalm 27:1 (KJV)

> I can do all things through Christ who strengthens me.
> —Philippians 4:13

Thank You, Jesus, that I have nothing to fear; You are the strength of my life. With You, there is nothing I face that I cannot overcome.

He that dwelleth in the secret place of the most High shall abide under the shadow of the Almighty. I will say of the LORD, He is my refuge and my fortress: my God; in him will I trust. Surely he shall deliver thee from the snare of the fowler, and from the noisome pestilence.

He shall cover thee with his feathers, and under his wings shalt thou trust: his truth shall be thy shield and buckler. Thou shalt not be afraid for the terror by night; nor for the arrow that flieth by day; Nor for the pestilence that walketh in darkness; nor for the destruction that wasteth at noonday.

A thousand shall fall at thy side, and ten thousand at thy right hand; but it shall not come nigh thee. Only with thine eyes shalt thou behold and see the reward of the wicked. Because thou hast made the Lord, which is my refuge, even the most High, thy habitation;

There shall no evil befall thee, neither shall any plague come nigh thy dwelling. For he shall give his angels charge over thee, to keep thee in all thy ways. They shall bear thee up in their hands, lest thou dash thy foot against a stone. Thou shalt tread upon the lion and adder: the young lion and the dragon shalt thou trample under feet.

Because he hath set his love upon me, therefore will I deliver him: I will set him on high, because he hath known my name. He shall call upon me, and I will answer him: I will be with him in trouble; I will deliver him, and honour him. With long life will I satisfy him, and shew him my salvation.

—PSALM 91 (KJV)

> Shew me thy ways, O LORD; teach me thy paths.
> Lead me in thy truth, and teach me: for thou art the
> God of my salvation; on thee do I wait all the day.
> —PSALM 25:4-5 (KJV)

Thank You, Jesus, no matter what the future holds, You will always be with me and keep me safe. Thank You I never have to be afraid.

> For I know the thoughts that I think toward you, says the LORD, thoughts of peace and not of evil, to give you a future and a hope. Then you will call upon Me and go and pray to Me, and I will listen to you. And you will seek Me and find Me, when you search for Me with all your heart.
> —JEREMIAH 29:11-13

> For God has not given us a spirit of fear, but of power and of love and of a sound mind.
> —2 TIMOTHY 1:7

> You will keep *him* in perfect peace,
> *Whose* mind *is* stayed *on You*,
> Because he trusts in You.
> —ISAIAH 26:3

Father, in Jesus' name, I choose not to worry about my future and the idea of getting married. Instead, I thank You that You will bring me and my mate together in Your timing. I thank You now for Your peace that keeps my heart and mind at rest as I trust in You. Thank You for working it all out for me.

> Delight yourself also in the LORD,
> And He shall give you the desires of your heart.
> —PSALM 37:4

Thank You, Jesus, that as I delight in You, You will bring me the desires of my heart. My future is in Your hands. I trust You are orchestrating Your will for my life.

PURITY

> It is God's will that you should be sanctified: that you should avoid sexual immorality; that each of you should learn to control his own body in a way that is holy and honorable, not in passionate lust like the heathen, who do not know God; For God did not call us to be impure, but to live a holy life.
> —1 THESSALONIANS 4:3-5,7 (NIV)

Father, Your Word has a high calling of holiness. Thank You for helping me meet that call with a grace to resist temptation and control my own body.

> If we confess our sins, he is faithful and just and will forgive us our sins and purify us from all unrighteousness.
> —1 JOHN 1:9-10 (NIV)

Father, thank You that Your Word promises forgiveness. I confess my sin to You now and accept Your forgiveness. Thank You for purifying my heart. I stand in Your presence free from guilt and condemnation. (Confess specific sins.)

> Great peace have those who love Your law,
> And nothing causes them to stumble.
> —Psalm 119:165

I love You and Your Word, Jesus. Thank You for giving me grace to not stumble. Thank You that my mind is free from torment.

> Blessed *are* the pure in heart,
> For they shall see God.
> —Matthew 5:8

Father, thank You for helping me stay pure in heart so I can see You.

> Since you have purified your souls in obeying the truth through the Spirit in sincere love of the brethren, love one another fervently with a pure heart.
> —1 Peter 1:22

Thank You, Jesus, that I love my brothers and sisters with a pure heart. Thank You that I have only pure thoughts towards others.

> How can a young man cleanse his way?
> By taking heed according to Your word.
> With my whole heart I have sought You;
> Oh, let me not wander from Your commandments!
> Your word I have hidden in my heart,
> That I might not sin against You!
> —Psalm 119:9-11

Father, I seek You with my whole heart and hide Your Word in me. Thank You for Your grace to obey You at all times so I may not sin against You.

DEPRESSION

My soul is among lions: and I lie even among them that are set on fire, even the sons of men, whose teeth are spears and arrows, and their tongue a sharp sword. Be thou exalted, O God, above the heavens; let thy glory be above all the earth.
They have prepared a net for my steps; my soul is bowed down: they have digged a pit before me, into the midst whereof they are fallen themselves. Selah.
My heart is fixed, O God, my heart is fixed: I will sing and give praise. Awake up, my glory; awake, psaltery and harp: I myself will awake early. I will praise thee, O LORD, among the people: I will sing unto thee among the nations.
—PSALM 57:4-9 (KJV)

But thou, O LORD, art a shield for me; my glory, and the lifter up of mine head.
—PSALM 3:3 (KJV)

Thank You, Jesus, that no matter what is happening around me, I can sing and give You praise! Thank You that I do not have to hang my head low because You are the glory and the lifter of my head.

> To comfort all who mourn,
> To console those who mourn in Zion,
> To give them beauty for ashes, the oil of joy for mourning,
> The garment of praise for the spirit of heaviness;
> That they may be called trees of righteousness,
> The planting of the Lord, that He may be glorified.
> —Isaiah 61:2b-3

> The thief does not come except to steal, and to kill, and to destroy. I have come that they may have life, and that they may have *it* more abundantly.
> —John 10:10

Thank You, Jesus, that You comfort me and exchange my mourning for Your joy. I shake off the spirit of heaviness and put on the garment of praise! I receive your abundant life now in Jesus' name.

> I drew them with gentle cords,
> With bands of love,
> And I was to them as those who take the yoke from their neck.
> I stooped *and* fed them.
> —Hosiah 11:4

Oh God, thank You for loving me so much and drawing me closer to You. Thank You for taking this yoke of depression off my life and filling me with Your peace.

They shall come with weeping, and with supplications will I lead them: I will cause them to walk by the rivers of waters in a straight way, wherein they shall not stumble: for I am a father to Israel, and Ephraim is my firstborn.
—Jeremiah 31:9 (kjv)

The Lord is my strength and my shield; my heart trusted in him, and I am helped: therefore my heart greatly rejoiceth; and with my song will I praise him. The Lord is their strength, and he is the saving strength of his anointed.
—Psalm 28:7-8 (kjv)

Weeping may endure for a night, but joy cometh in the morning.
—Psalm 30:5b (kjv)

Father, though I weep, I come to You knowing that You will lead me to rivers of life. Thank You for turning my tears of sadness into tears of joy! You are my strength and I trust in You. My heart rejoices when I think of Your goodness.

I will praise You, O Lord, with my whole heart;
I will tell of all Your marvelous works.
I will be glad and rejoice in You;
I will sing praise to Your name, O Most High.
—Psalm 9:1-2

There is no one like the God of Jeshurun,
Who rides the heavens to help you,
And in His excellency on the clouds.
The eternal God *is your* refuge,
And underneath *are* the everlasting arms.
—Deuteronomy 33:26-27a

God, I follow David's example and choose to praise You with my whole heart. I know if my heart is full of praise, there will be no room for depression. God, You are an awesome God and I run to You for refuge. Thank You for hiding me in Your arms and restoring unto me a glad heart.

Loneliness

> The LORD your God is with you,
>   he is mighty to save.
> He will take great delight in you,
>   he will quiet you with his love,
>   he will rejoice over you with singing.
> —Zephaniah 3:17 (NIV)

> Never will I leave you; never will I forsake you.
> —Hebrews 13:5b (NIV)

God, sometimes I am so lonely it hurts. Thank You for helping me understand how much You love me. Thank You, Jesus, for being with me wherever I go. Help me live with awareness that I am never truly alone.

> And you are complete in Him, who is the head of all principality and power.
> —Colossians. 2:10

Thank You, Jesus, that I am not looking for my better half. I am complete in You!

> Look carefully then how you walk! Live purposefully *and* worthily *and* accurately, not as the unwise *and* witless, but as wise (sensible, intelligent people),
> Making the very most of the time [buying up each opportunity], because the days are evil.
> —EPHESIANS 5:15-16 (AMP)

Father, thank You that I have purpose in life and You give me the ability to live wisely. Instead of sitting around feeling lonely, I am going to make the most of this time and do something productive. Thank You for helping me develop good friendships.

DISCOURAGEMENT

> May our Lord Jesus Christ himself and God our Father who loved us and by his grace gave us eternal encouragement and good hope, encourage your hearts and strengthen you in every good deed and word.
> —2 THESSALONIANS 2:16-17 (NIV)

Thank You, Father for encouraging me with Your love. I receive Your strength to overcome discouragement, now, in Jesus' name.

> My soul is weary with sorrow;
> strengthen me according to your word.
> —PSALM 119:28 (NIV)

> I have set the LORD always before me;
> Because *He is* at my right hand I shall not be moved.
> Therefore my heart is glad, and my glory rejoices;
> My flesh also will rest in hope.
> —PSALM 16:8-9

Thank You, Jesus, as I read and declare Your Word my soul is strengthened and infused with Your presence. Instead of looking at my circumstances, I choose to set my eyes on You knowing that You love me.

> For You, LORD, have made me glad through Your work;
> I will triumph in the works of Your hands.
> O LORD, how great are Your works!
> Your thoughts are very deep.
>
> —PSALM 92:4-5

Thank You, Jesus, for giving me grace to get my eyes off myself and onto You and Your good works. When I think of all You have done for me, I get happy and very grateful!

> For it is God who works in you both to will and to do for *His* good pleasure. Do all things without complaining and disputing.
>
> —PHILIPPIANS 2:13-14

Thank You, Jesus, for doing a divine work in me. I know You are not finished with me yet, but it encourages me to know You never give up on changing me into Your likeness. I choose to be grateful and not complain.

RECEIVING FORGIVENESS

> In Him we have redemption through His blood, the forgiveness of sins, according to the riches of His grace.
>
> —EPHESIANS 1:7

> For He made Him who knew no sin *to be* sin for us, that we might become the righteousness of God in Him.
> —2 Corinthians 5:21

Thank You, Jesus, for paying the price for my sin. You were the perfect Lamb slain for my transgression and through You I am righteous in God.

> If we confess our sins, He is faithful and just to forgive us *our* sins and to cleanse us from all unrighteousness.
> —1 John 1:9

Thank You, Jesus, that Your Word promises forgiveness. I confess my sin to You now and receive Your forgiveness and cleansing power. (Confess your specific sins.)

> For though a righteous *man* falls seven times, he rises again, but the wicked are brought down by calamity.
> —Proverbs 24:16 (NIV)

Lord, I repent of my sin. Thank You, Jesus, for forgiving me no matter how many times I fall short of Your glory. I will get up and appropriate Your grace to grow beyond this weakness.

> When I kept silence, my bones waxed old through my roaring all the day long. For day and night thy hand was heavy upon me: my moisture is turned into the drought of summer. Selah.
> I acknowledged my sin unto thee, and mine iniquity have I not hid. I said, I will confess my transgressions unto the LORD; and thou forgavest the iniquity of my sin. Selah.
>
> —PSALM 32:3-5 (KJV)

> For You, LORD, *are* good, and ready to forgive,
> And abundant in mercy to all those who call upon You.
>
> —PSALM 86:5

Thank You, Jesus, that I can let it all hang out with You and You are always ready to forgive me. I hold nothing back knowing You love me. Thank You, Jesus, for Your mercy. Thank You for washing away guilt and shame.

> The steps of a good man are ordered by the LORD: and he delighteth in his way. Though he fall, he shall not be utterly cast down: for the LORD upholdeth him with his hand.
>
> —PSALM 37:23-24 (KJV)

Thank You, Lord, for holding my hand like a father holds his child's hand walking across the street. Even though I may get tripped up on life's streets of temptation, You hold me up so I do not utterly fall.

GIVING FORGIVENESS

"And whenever you stand praying, if you have anything against anyone, forgive him, that your Father in heaven may also forgive you your trespasses. But if you do not forgive, neither will your Father in heaven forgive your trespasses."
—Mark 11:25-26

Then Peter came to Him and said, "Lord, how often shall my brother sin against me, and I forgive him? Up to seven times?" Jesus said to him, "I do not say to you, up to seven times, but up to seventy times seven.
—Matthew 18:21-22

And forgive us our debts, as we forgive our debtors.
—Matthew 6:12 (KJV)

God, forgive me for holding unforgiveness in my heart. I ask for Your grace now to give me the ability to forgive others. Right now, I choose to forgive _____ and release him/her from any debt I feel owed me. I do not care what he/she has done to me or how many times he/she has hurt me. Right now, I choose to love him/her and pray blessings over his/her life. (Repeat this prayer for as many people you need to forgive.)

Your Future Mate

And the LORD God formed man of the dust of the ground, and breathed into his nostrils the breath of life; and man became a living being. But for Adam there was not found a helper comparable to him. And the LORD God caused a deep sleep to fall on Adam, and he slept: and He took one of his ribs, and closed up the flesh in its place. Then the rib which the LORD God had taken from man He made into a woman, and He brought her to the man.

—Genesis 2:7, 20b-22

Women

Father, in Jesus' name, I thank You for creating a man especially for me. Thank You for preparing him to be the man of God you have called him to be. In Your timing, bring me to him in a special way. As we get to know each other, give us both a knowing that we are called to marry and be partners for life. Prepare me to be the best helpmeet for him that I can possible be.

Men

Father, in Jesus' name, I thank You for handcrafting a woman especially for me. I believe You will bring her to me in Your timing. Thank You for preparing her to be the helper You have called her to be. I pray, when we meet and get to know each other, we will both know without a doubt that You have called us to marry and be partners for life. Lord, prepare me to be the man of God I need to be, so I can be the best husband possible.

Closing Prayer

Thank You, Jesus, that my future is in Your hands. I trust You are orchestrating my future according to your will and in that I rest. I will not torture myself trying to figure it all out.

I know You love me and want what is best for me. Forgive me for not trusting You completely. Thank You for Your grace to enable me to release my future desires and wait patiently on Your timing. I choose to stop asking "When, God, when?" I will not allow my unknown future to rob my present joy. In You I am complete. In You I am fulfilled.

Thank You for helping me, by Your grace, enjoy my single years and every journey of life. I live and move and have my being in You. It is You I live for; You are my life!

Thank You, Jesus, for all You do for me and all You have planned for me. Thank You I have a wonderful future. I do not know what the future holds, but I know Who holds the future. I trust You, God, with my whole heart.

Even though I thought for sure I'd be married by now, I choose to live for You and enjoy every day of my life.

Thank You for loving me!

About the Author

Jeff Hidden is an international speaker and president of Mighty River Ministries based in Atlanta, Georgia. Jeff's powerful teaching ministry emphasizes victory for the Believer through wisdom, character, and intimacy with the Lord. His dream is to see Christians live like Christ in order to attract people to Jesus.

In addition to Jeff teaching God's Word on Sundays for churches across America and other nations, Mighty River Ministries has a special branch dedicated to helping singles of all ages in the area of relationships.

Jeff's unique seminar on relationships has been translated into Finnish and Spanish and has been heard by multitudes in America, England, Africa, Mexico, and Finland.

Jeff is married to Pippa and together they are proud parents of two daughters—Moriah and Jessica.

For more information visit www.mightyriver.org

Special Offer

"I Thought For Sure I'd Be Married By Now" is taken from a lesson taught in Jeff Hidden's unique, life-changing seminar on relationships called "Christian Dating? Raising A Standard!" Thousands across America and other nations including England, Finland, Mexico, and Zimbabwe have been ministered to by this powerful seminar. Topics include:

- How to raise a biblical standard in relationships.

- Finding your mate God's way, including insight on how to avoid wrong and hurtful relationships in the process.

- Keys in evaluating a potential mate. *Is he or she the right one?*

- Healing from past broken relationships and how to enjoy your single years.

- So you found Mr. or Miss Right, now what?

Package includes:
1. Six 45-minute lessons
2. Seminar manual
3. Covenant of Chastity
4. *Raising A Standard!* ink pen

Cassette ... $30.00   CD ... $36.00   VHS Video ... $59.00
• Add $3.00 for Shipping & Handling

The videos are great for Singles' Sunday School, Home Groups, and Bible Studies.

"Our singles group watched Jeff's video series "Christian Dating? Raising a Standard!" and it ministered to us in a powerful way.

Jeff's understanding in the area of Godly relationships is amazing. With his practical, and many times humorous, way of teaching, Jeff seized our attention and God seized our hearts. I recommend every Singles Ministry to make this an annual curriculum for their group."

Additional Comments

"Your seminar has literally changed my life. I am healed of my past and now have a hope-filled future! I have learned how to enjoy the journey of waiting for my mate."

"It's so practical! Jeff knows how to make it so clear. I laughed, I cried, I learned...I was changed."

"I wish I would have heard this 10 years ago!"

For more information or to order with credit card call:
(770) 7-WISDOM
(MasterCard, Visa, Discover Card)

Or, send check payable to Mighty River Ministries:
PO Box 2196, Kennesaw, GA 30156

For more information on this seminar and many other seminars taught by Jeff Hidden, go to:
www.mightyriver.org.

Additional Teaching Series Available

Jeff Hidden has traveled and taught God's Word across America and in other nations. Here is a sample of teaching series available through Jeff's ministry. For a complete list of teaching materials go to www.mightyriver.org.

1. What Are Friends for Anyway? 3-Part Series

The three most important things in life are: 1. Relationships 2. Relationships, and 3. Relationships. We all have a need and a desire for true friends. If you want to have good friends, you must learn how to become one yourself. In this series, you will learn God's idea of true friendship and how you can develop meaningful and fulfilling relationships. God says, *"...two are better than one."*

Cassette...$15.00   CD...$18.00

2. What to Do in the Meantime 3-Part Series

You have prayed and your answer, dream or vision has not come yet...*What do you do?* Learn how to enjoy where you are on the way to where you are going. Discover what *God* is doing in the meantime and when your miracle will come. A life-changing series on how not to allow unmet desires distract you from enjoying the journeys of life.

Cassette...$15.00   CD...$18.00

3. How to Walk in God's Wisdom 5-Part Series

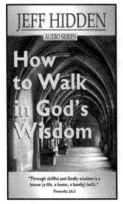

Have you ever wondered what Jesus would do in your situation? Are you at a crossroads? What you need is wisdom. In this insightful series, you will discover there is more to God's wisdom then simply getting an answer. Learn how to go beyond getting an answer from God to actually becoming wise. As you become wise, you will make more right choices, avoid pitfalls in life, and reach your full potential in Christ!

Cassette...$25.00   CD...$30.00

4. Characteristics of a 'Real' Christian 2-Part Series

This series is designed to 'raise the standard' of what it means to be a Christian. Paul says if a person wants to be a leader for God, he or she must exemplify certain characteristics of true Christianity. What are those character qualities? How does one develop them in his or her life? This series will help you become more like Christ and be able to identify His qualities in others. In light of finding a Godly mate, you will want to know if he or she is a 'real' Christian!

Cassette...$10.00   CD...$12.00